Pat –

Thanks so much for
Reading! Enjoy!

Much Love,

Somewhere
Unexpected

Suzanne Glidewell

Print ISBN: 978-1-54398-693-8

eBook ISBN: 978-1-54398-694-5

THOMAS

After Easter, it seemed like I saw less and less of Maura. I attempted to schedule meeting-up for a run a few times, and even invited her to one of my family's Sunday dinners after much goading from my mother and sister. Her response was consistent; she would love to, but she had plans with Ethan. I was surprised that she was spending so much time with him after she'd confessed she wasn't ready to meet his family and her awkward reaction to seeing him when he surprised her at work. Of course, her awkward reaction could have had something to do with the fact that I had very obviously been considering making a move on her right before Ethan showed up.

Ultimately, I was glad I hadn't been stupid enough to try anything on her. It had clearly been a moment of loneliness and weakness on my part. Not that trying to get laid was a sign of weakness – but it was when you were stupid enough to consider trying to get it from a prude like Maura just because she was kind and helped you with your unresolved father-son issues.

I still saw her on Wednesdays when I volunteered. She would even pop into to the garage on days when it was Sydney's turn to supervise, usually within the first hour. I noticed her behavior followed a pattern: she always started off reserved when she first arrived, but within fifteen minutes, she was back to joking with me like nothing had changed. Then she ended each day by asking how I was. The look in her eyes told me she was really asking about any aspects of grief I was still dealing with surrounding my dad's death. I felt like I was being honest when I told her I was okay.

Truthfully, the feelings of anger and frustration I used to have whenever a memory of my dad came up weren't there anymore. Well, at least not as intensely as they had been before. I could now be alone in my parents' house without that old feeling of uneasiness.

I didn't tell Maura this, but I had taken her insight about guilt and decided to channel it into being a better son to my mom by fixing things around the house or taking her out to do things that my father had hated to do, like going to museums or the movies. I'd even started going to mass with her occasionally, but honestly, I also always hoped to see Maura when I went.

Naturally, I had always been a momma's boy, so this was an easy role to step into, but I still had several years of being a selfish asshole to make-up for. In all honesty, I didn't know if my actions were really that altruistic because I was starting to prefer my family's company over my friends like Tyler and Jeremy and the flock of hoes they usually hung out with.

Now that the anger and guilt about my relationship with my father was subsiding gradually, my brain was flooded with questions about what happens when a person dies. I suppose I had always thought the idea of heaven sounded nice, but as I had gotten older, the logic didn't seem to add up. But I didn't like the idea of my dad being dead and there being nothing more to it. Life seemed kind of pointless if this was all there was.

I wasn't really yearning for a philosophical conversation about life and death with anyone. I knew what my family thought: my dad's soul was in purgatory and would eventually make it to heaven – which was why my mom felt the need to go to mass most days, believing the more she prayed, the quicker he would get into heaven. I knew this gave my mom a sense of comfort, so I was not about to debate the subject with her.

I was interested in what Maura thought and whether her beliefs were as traditional as my mom's, or if there was some variation that seemed less superstitious. But it wasn't something I was just going to bring up casually at the end of a Wednesday night. I wasn't even sure that there was ever a right time to bring it up with anybody. But if I were to ever talk to anyone about it, she would be the one I'd talk to...what an odd designation to have for a person.

I pulled into the driveway of the University District Youth Center, knowing that it was Maura's turn to be out in the garage with me. I had grown fond of Sydney, too, but it was more entertaining to tease Maura during the two hours of instruction. Maura provided way more material than Sydney because she knew absolutely nothing about cars, mechanical operations, or even physics in general. She wasn't afraid to show it, either, as evidenced by the random questions she would always blurt out. I suspected that she put herself in that position so that the others didn't feel stupid for not knowing something. That seemed like the kind of thing she would do: make other people feel better even if it meant making herself look clueless.

I went into the garage and examined where we had left off on the engine of the Corolla. It was clearly cracked. The kids had diagnosed the blown gasket last week, with my help ruling out other things. We had flushed the coolant and replaced the oil and put sealer on it. Today we were going to see if that had fixed the problem. I knew it wouldn't fix anything because the gasket and the head were warped beyond repair. I had already ordered the gasket and flat that needed to be replaced. Of course, I wanted them to follow the steps of evaluating potential solutions before just telling them the answer.

I glanced up from under the hood to see Maura standing in front of the garage, sipping coffee. She had been so quiet I hadn't heard her walk up, and now she was staring off into the distance, lost in thought.

"Hey," I greeted her. She blinked her eyes and looked over at me. She nodded but didn't say anything. A silence passed as I went to pull out the tools we'd use that day. She was watching me.

"I didn't realize I was so entertaining to watch," I commented, snapping her out of her daze.

"Sorry, I guess I've just hit my afternoon lull," she explained, taking a step inside the garage.

"No food or drink in the workspace."

"But this is my afternoon pick-me-up," she argued. "It's so I can stay alert throughout your riveting program and provide ample feedback. Otherwise your boring voice would just make me fall asleep."

"Sorry, but it says clearly on that fantastic sign you made me put up: 'No food or drink in the workspace.'" I pointed at the laminated sign she had made after insisting I generate rules with the group as an activity.

She frowned, wanting me to make an exception for her.

"Maura, you're Catholic; don't you just live for following rules?"

"Fine. Is this an acceptable location to consume my beverage?" she asked in a put-out voice, stepping just outside the garage.

"Maybe take another step back, just to be safe," I suggested, curious to see if she would do it.

As predicted, she complied. It didn't really matter if she drank her coffee inside the garage since she wasn't going to be touching anything, but giving her a hard time was one of my favorite things to do. Plus, it seemed to move her more quickly past the new pattern of being so reserved with me. I went back to setting out tools.

"So, how was your day? Fix any cracked heads? Flush any coolants? Change some oils?"

"Good job paying attention in class," I said condescendingly. "Yes, those are all things that a mechanic does. But I worked on a transmission all day."

"Ah, yes...I hope it was received well," she said in a serious tone, but clearly making a pun. The fact that she maintained a straight face made me smile.

"You are such a nerd," I sighed.

She shrugged and took a sip of her drink, looking pleased with herself. Over her shoulder I saw Father Sean walking toward the garage. He was not wearing his white robe, but instead was dressed in jeans and a zip-up fleece, looking like he could blend in as a regular guy.

"Hey, Thomas," he greeted before I could warn Maura. She turned and saw him approach.

"Maura." He nodded hello.

"Aren't your Newmanites volunteering inside with the clothes closet and the art group?" she asked, hinting that he shouldn't be in the garage.

"And the kitchen," he added, not catching on. "But I thought it'd be great to come by and check out how things are going out here so that I can tell the Warrens and the Paulsons all about it on Sunday. You don't mind if I sit in, do you, Thomas?"

"Nope, not at all."

I honestly didn't mind. I knew being around Father Sean annoyed Maura, but I thought he was a decent guy. I had always thought of priests as super serious and had never been able to picture them having a normal conversation with anyone. However, my interactions with Father Sean had countered that stereotype. It was too bad that Maura couldn't still be dating him instead of that Ethan guy. I couldn't understand how someone as easygoing as her could be interested in someone as stuffy as Ethan.

"Great, so what're you guys working on?" Father Sean asked enthusiastically.

It seemed that everyone had gotten their coffee that afternoon but me.

"Maura, how about you share what we've been working on?" I asked for my own amusement.

She gave me a pointed look.

"Well, there's a blown gasket that they tried to seal. My suggestion that it might be the flux capacitor has been shut down."

"And how many times has that idea been suggested and shut down, Maura?" I asked, wanting Father Sean to know the ridiculousness I was dealing with.

"Oh, only like four, maybe five times," she said nonchalantly.

Father Sean turned to Maura. "Clearly there's not enough money in the budget for plutonium, or he would've given more consideration to your suggestion," he humored her.

It started to make sense why they had dated.

"I just don't want anyone to come back and say he totally 'Biffed' it."

Father Sean laughed a genuine laugh, which surprised me, given that the joke was groan-worthy.

She looked over at me. "I'm glad somebody appreciates how clever I am."

"Is that what we're calling it now?"

She glared playfully and threw her coffee cup away.

"If you'll excuse me, I'm going to round up the group," she announced coolly while walking away.

Father Sean stepped into the garage to look under the hood of the car.

"So, are you liking it so far?" he inquired, looking down.

"Yeah," I said. "It's been good."

A silence passed.

"That sealer's not going to work, is it?"

"No, but they don't know that yet."

"Yeah, it looks like the head is warped pretty badly," he observed, looking to me to verify that he was correct.

"Yep," I nodded.

He looked proud of himself.

Maura came through the back door, followed by the usual group of teenagers. Once they assembled, I noticed Justin and Eric were missing. Maura pulled Father Sean into the corner to sit up on the counter where she and Sydney usually positioned themselves.

I was surprised how comfortable I felt, even with Father Sean observing me. It helped that the group and I were on a roll that day; everyone was participating, answering questions, and generating ideas on how to test things out and fix the problem – which was probably why I was caught completely off guard when I heard the backdoor to the main building slam and curse words being yelled.

I looked up to see Justin charging towards the garage. I froze mid-sentence. Maura immediately hopped down from the counter and went out to approach him. Since Justin was over twice her size, I didn't think this was the best idea. I looked over at Father Sean, who seemed to have the same thought because he had gotten down to follow Maura.

Maura stood in front of Justin, who was still yelling, "Where the fuck is he?! I'm gonna fucking beat his ass! Motherfucker!"

He looked past her, frantically trying to find out who was in the garage. I walked towards them, feeling the need to protect Maura.

"Justin, Justin," she said calmly and firmly. She was holding her palms up, her body language encouraging him to calm down. She somehow sensed we were walking up behind her.

"It's fine, Sean. Thomas, get back to what you were doing," she said, using the same tone with us.

Her strong demeanor led me to believe that she had everything under control, despite my better judgment. Father Sean reached the same conclusion and backed off. I returned to the garage, but I could still hear her exchange with Justin.

"Justin, look at me, look at me. What's going on? Why are you so pissed?"

"Fucking lying-ass motherfucker!" he shouted.

I tried to get the rest of the kids to focus back on me, but obviously the drama outside was far more interesting.

"I know, I get it, you're fucking upset," she validated.

"Fucking Eric!" he screamed. He was now pacing, but no longer looked like he was going to storm the garage.

"Okay," she responded calmly, standing still. "Eric's not here. So you don't have to worry about kicking his ass." Her tone was slow and matter-of-fact.

He let out another scream, his fists were still clenched, but he was pacing at a slower rate. He turned and walked with purpose towards the main building. Maura followed behind him slowly, still looking amazingly calm.

Justin leaned face-first against the wall and started to pound the wall with his fist. He wasn't exactly punching the wall, but he still looked angry, though not quite as unpredictable as he had a few seconds ago. Maura turned back to the garage. She motioned to Father Sean without saying anything, and he responded by closing the garage door, blocking Maura and Justin from everyone's view.

I was disappointed in myself for not thinking of that sooner when I had tried to regain everyone's attention. However, I still didn't like the idea of leaving Maura out there alone, regardless of how much experience she had with her job. Father Sean continued to stand in the back and occasionally look out the window, which provided me some peace of mind.

I fumbled through the rest of the meeting, distracted by the earlier interruption and the fact that Maura hadn't returned. We weren't able to run the car since the garage door was closed, so I just let them know that we would be replacing the gasket and the head next week. I had twenty minutes left to kill, and I resorted to doing something I never thought I would ever do: use Maura's "What's Your Favorite?" game.

I tried to keep it to cars but quickly realized none of them had ever had a car, so I ended up turning it over to them. They seemed familiar with the activity, having worked with Maura for a while. I know I had teased her mercilessly about her filling silence this way, but I probably learned more about those four kids in the twenty minutes we spent playing the game than I had in the rest of the times I'd spent with them combined. They even pulled Father Sean into it, too. Before I knew it, the atmosphere of the group had transformed from the unexpected tension that had erupted earlier into one that was laughing and calm.

I opened the door and dismissed them, glad that it had happened, but disappointed Maura had missed it. I turned to find

Father Sean still standing around. I worried I was going to get negative feedback about how I had frozen.

"So, that was an eventful day," he let out a slight laugh. "Anything like that ever happen before?"

"Nope," I said simply.

He sighed and shook his head. He wasn't looking at me, but instead seemed to be processing what had happened.

"Well, despite the interruption, I thought it was really great. I'm so grateful you agreed to do this."

I just nodded.

"I mean, you're really great at what you do. So, thank you again."

I nodded again and let a silence pass. I was never good at receiving compliments, but I forced myself to say something.

"It's good to be helping. I appreciate the opportunity." When the words came out of my mouth I didn't recognize myself.

"Are you going to be heading out to Latona tonight?"

It took a second to register what he was referring to, but then I realized it was Wednesday and he was talking about the young adult group.

"No, I have some guys out tomorrow, so I have to head into the shop early." I made my excuse but decided there was no sense in making him think I would ever be back to Latona with the Blessed Sacrament crowd. "I haven't been out there since the last time you saw me there."

"I know," he responded quickly. "I just hoped maybe there would be somebody there I could talk baseball with instead of encyclicals," he laughed.

I turned off the lights to the garage and pulled down the door.

"Actually," he said as I went to lock the garage, "the Warrens gave me their tickets to Saturday's game. You interested?"

"M's versus Red Sox?"

"Yeah, I don't know why Harold didn't want to go. Crazy, right? Especially since Felix is going to kick their asses."

I couldn't believe I was making plans with a priest to go to a baseball game on a Saturday night, but his last sentence almost made me forget that he was a priest.

"Sure."

"Great. Meet at the south entrance around five thirty?"

I nodded.

"Are you heading out now?" he asked.

"Um, I think I'm going to check in with Maura, before I go," I said, but stopped before explaining my reasoning behind it. He smiled knowingly.

"Sure, sure, sounds good. Just know, she's been doing this for a while. She's a lot tougher than she looks," he informed me. He then held out his hand and I shook it. "Once again, you're doing a great job, Thomas. I'll see you Saturday."

He walked off to the front entrance of the building to meet up with the other volunteers. I wanted to know how the rest of the interaction with Justin had unfolded because I wanted to know that everything was okay with him, but I did have to admit, like Father Sean suspected, my interest was mostly because I wanted to be sure that Maura was okay. I knew it was silly to be concerned for her, given how calm and collected her reaction had been. But I couldn't shake the feeling that I needed to see her before I left.

I went inside the main building and saw the doorway to Maura's office open with the light on. When I peered in, I saw her sitting by herself, typing away. I gently knocked on the door.

"Hey," she said quietly. She smiled but looked exhausted. "How'd the rest of the afternoon go?"

"Fine." I stepped inside but remained standing. "I just wanted to make sure everything was okay before I took off." It would have been more honest to ask her if she, specifically, was okay.

She sighed. "Yes. It took some time, but Mr. Justin was able to calm down." She rubbed her hands over her face, like she was trying to wake herself up. "And I was able to get more information about why he was so pissed at Eric. Once we track Eric down, or if we're able to, we'll make sure they meet with both Sydney and me before they come back to you, and they'll fill out a safety contract," she assured me.

This hadn't really crossed my mind as a concern.

"Sorry you had to see him like that. We haven't seen anything like that in a long time, but I guess it was just the perfect storm today," she shared without giving away too much information.

"I'm sorry I couldn't have been more helpful."

"No, you were plenty helpful." She motioned at the chair by her desk for me to sit down. "Trust me, there were about a thousand ways you could have made it worse."

"So, you normally take on guys twice your size?"

She shook her head and laughed.

"I'm serious, someday I might need protection out there on the mean streets of Seattle," I joked when what I really meant to tell her was that I was highly impressed by her ability to manage a situation like the one I had seen. Frankly, it would have terrified me if I had been in her shoes.

"Most of the time, a pissed-off person just needs to be told that you can tell they're pissed off. And anyway, I've known Justin long enough to know he wasn't going to do anything to me. I'm sorry I had to bail on you like that."

I couldn't believe after how emotionally drained I imagined she must be, she was apologizing to me. Naturally, I made light of it, because I didn't know what else to do.

"Well, I don't want to make you too jealous, but I did lead the group in a roaring game of 'What's Your Favorite?' for the last twenty minutes."

"What?" she exclaimed loudly, throwing her head back dramatically, but smiling. "I missed 'What's Your Favorite?' Urgh! Now I'm officially upset." She sighed and smiled at me, slightly disguising her exhaustion.

"So, are you almost done here, or are you going to have to stay late?" I pointed towards her monitor.

She briefly glanced at it, then back at me. "Yeah, he ended up sharing a lot of other stuff that has to be recorded and followed up on." She looked back at her computer, silently taking inventory for a moment. "But no police report, so that's a good thing...yay." She turned back to me.

"Pollyanna strikes again," I teased her. "Are you going to need dinner or something?"

"No, I'm good. I should be done in the next hour or so. I'll have time to grab something from the fridge before mass. Why are you always trying to feed me?"

"I guess it's my mother's side in me coming out. We're Italian; we perpetually want to feed people."

"Does that mean if you're half Irish, you perpetually want to drink too?"

"You know how it is, McCormick," I retorted.

"After the day I've had, I can say I really do," she joked and then paused, knowing she needed to get back to work in order to make it to mass on time.

"Well," I started the goodbye so she wouldn't have to kick me out, "I will let you get to your work and I will see you next week." I stood up. "Have a good night."

"You too," she said before turning back to her computer to resume typing. I walked myself out. I wondered if going to mass and whatever she had with Ethan was enough to redeem her day. I hoped it was, but the cynic in me doubted it.

MAURA

I scarfed down a Cup of Noodles while I shut down my computer at six forty. I had already texted Ethan to tell him not to pick me up but instead meet me at the church. It seemed like the incident report I was filling out for Justin kept going on and on, given all the information he'd shared with me.

It turned out that his anger at Eric was just the tip of the iceberg. I had worked with Justin for over two years and he was currently in the reunification process with his mom, which we had all thought was going fine. Apparently not.

Justin confessed he hadn't been staying with his mom because he didn't like her drug-dealing boyfriend who had moved in. But he was still occasionally hanging out there.

Shit hit the fan the previous night when Justin went to his mom's and was accused of stealing five thousand dollars' worth of drugs. Justin wouldn't go into detail, not even giving me the boyfriend's name, because he knew I would've filed a police report on top of telling his CPS worker. He was terrified of the police from previous experiences. He told me his mom had taken the boyfriend's side and kicked him out. Justin was convinced Eric was the one who had taken the drugs because of things Eric had said two nights earlier when he was with him at the apartment, hence the dramatic entrance into the garage that afternoon.

I'd lucked out that his CPS worker had been available when I called that afternoon and had driven over before Justin decided to run. We convinced him that going into emergency foster care was a safer option than the streets, given that the boyfriend was probably looking for him. It wasn't a permanent solution, but it was enough for the moment.

I slipped into Mass just after the procession. Ethan had texted me where he was sitting before I got there. I would have liked to sit with just him, but of course he was sitting with a group of the young adults. I wanted to be at Mass after the day I'd had, knowing it would make me feel better, but the thought of going to Latona with everyone afterwards was not appealing. Then again, the alcohol might make it worthwhile, so in the end, I agreed.

Ethan suggested following me back to my apartment so I could drop off my car. That way we'd only have to find one parking spot by the bar and he could just take me home afterwards. I was a huge fan of this plan because it meant I could have more than one drink...oh, and Ethan was being chivalrous, too.

We got to the bar after everyone else.

Ethan started up a conversation with a couple of the other guys about how universal healthcare legislation was anti-Catholic. If it had been a different day, I might have challenged some of their points because a lot of them were propaganda and not fact-based, but I didn't really have the energy that night. They probably wouldn't have taken my points seriously anyway. As I was zoning out and appreciating my Hefeweizen, Sean pulled up a chair next to me.

"Hey, McCormick, how's it going?" he called me out of my daze.

"Good," I sighed, hoping he was just doing a standard greeting and would move on quickly.

"So, did everything end up okay for that kid?"

"Uh, yeah, everything's fine," I humored him with the easiest answer.

"What about you? You okay?"

"Yeah, I'll be fine."

It had been a rough day, but it wasn't anything I hadn't encountered before. I knew that despite the current setback, Justin could bounce back from it. That was the peace that came from believing in resiliency.

"See, that's what I told Thomas," he said. "You're a lot tougher than you look. You do look like you need a refill though," he commented on my empty glass. "I'm heading up if you want to join me."

He must have known I didn't want to hear the conversation that was taking place next to me. I followed him to the bar and let him order for me, which could have been a mistake, since he handed me a Jameson and Ginger. I was surprised he had ordered liquor, but also that he remembered my go-to cocktail. I looked at him for an explanation.

"Some days warrant some whiskey at the end of them," he clinked his pint glass to my highball.

I took a sip. It tasted like a double, but that could've been because I hadn't had liquor in a long time.

"Thomas is doing an awesome job. Don't you think?" he said.

"Yeah, it's good you used your priest privilege to avoid working in the clothes closet with the lowly lay volunteers so you could sit and evaluate another volunteer's work today."

I took another sip.

"And here I thought I had successfully avoided getting crap from you," he smiled.

I tried to not remember what it was like to kiss him, but it was always difficult when he smiled that way.

"Is it called 'giving someone crap' or is it called 'holding someone accountable?'" I tilted my head at him.

"Touché."

He turned to face me, leaning on the bar, propping himself up on his elbow.

"So, it's like a real thing with Ethan now?" Sean nodded over at him before looking back at me.

He was trying to read me. When I was twenty this had been endearing; now it was annoying.

"Yes, we're dating," I answered, anticipating the conversation was going to have some sort of overprotective big brother feel to it.

"Is it serious?"

"Yeah."

I reflected on how Ethan had told me he loved me for the first time five days ago. I'd responded by saying I loved him back. Maybe I wasn't a hundred percent sure I did, but I was about eighty percent sure, so I rounded up. I mean, he was smart and thoughtful and – most importantly – a devout Catholic. I knew if I wasn't completely in love with him now I would be eventually. To be fair, the only other relationships where I had said 'I love you' were my high school boyfriend and Sean, and I didn't think either were the best comparison against which to measure.

My relationship with my high school boyfriend, Ian, was mostly based on comfort and friendship. And then with Sean, everything had been so emotionally charged: a stars-in-your-eyes, head-over-heels situation. With Ethan, everything was calculated, logical, and controlled. I was starting to resign myself to the idea that these were the hallmarks of a true adult relationship that would be the foundation for a good marriage. Passion faded. Respect and commitment were what really mattered. If I got too hung up on immature shit like waiting to have more butterflies in my stomach, Ethan might move on to the next willing woman, and there were several to choose from.

"What's your favorite thing about him?" he asked, mimicking my get-to-know-you game.

"He's not discerning the priesthood," I retorted.

"You happy?"

I raised an eyebrow at Sean, wondering why he would ask me that.

"Yes, why?"

"Just making sure."

He took a sip of his beer. I could tell by his tone that he didn't believe me.

"You know, if I'd said half the things he's been saying tonight about universal healthcare while we were dating, you would've been a lot more vocal than you're being now. In fact, I think the term, 'rip me a new one' comes to mind."

"So?" I remained nonchalant, despite knowing that what he said was true.

I wanted to declare that my passivity was only due to the overwhelming afternoon I had. But Sean's observation reminded me of the barbecue Ethan and I had gone to the previous weekend. There had been a discussion, or rather a group rant, about public schools damaging the morality of all children, and the increased need for Catholics to homeschool or send their kids to Catholic school. I discovered that Ethan strongly believed this.

Being the product of public school, and the daughter of two public school teachers, I disagreed. It wasn't that I was against Catholic schools or homeschooling, I just was supportive of public schools and didn't necessarily see them as something a person needed to protect their children from. Normally, I wouldn't let being the minority opinion stop me from voicing my perspective, but I stayed silent. If Ethan was really that passionate about his future children accessing a Catholic education, who was I to challenge that? I mean, if the relationship ended in marriage, compromises would have to be made. Thankfully, there was no way for Sean to know what had happened at the barbecue, so I felt I was safe in acting like I didn't know what he was talking about.

"Just wondering if your opinions have changed or if you've changed."

I gave him a questioning look.

"Either you agree with the stuff he and the other guys are saying, which I highly doubt, or you don't talk about what you believe in anymore."

"Or I've gotten older and I know a losing fight when I see one. It's unfortunate I didn't have that wisdom back then," I said coolly.

"So you see your relationship with Ethan as a losing fight?" he asked in an equally cool manner.

"That's not what – you're putting words in my mouth," I argued poorly. I might as well have just exclaimed 'Nun-uh!'

He didn't say anything, letting his point resonate.

"Look, I had a shitty day, so whatever point you have, just make it," I said bluntly.

"Does Ethan know you had a shitty day?"

"Well, it's not like I can tell him details."

"Doesn't matter. He should know just by looking at you, regardless of whatever joke or smile you throw out there. If the relationship is that serious, and he's really put the effort into knowing you, he should know just by looking at you. He should know that the last thing you need is to be here right now with a bunch of people so clueless as to how comfortable their lives really are, debating issues without knowing how bad other people, kids in their own backyard, have it. And I'm just wondering why he doesn't know that? I'm wondering what else he doesn't know about you?"

"God, Sean, it's only been a few months," I underplayed how serious the relationship was. "I'm sorry if I haven't told him everything about myself within the first three dates like I did with you when I was young and stupid."

"After a while, I'm not going to be a valid excuse for being guarded. And you're going to have to ask yourself why you're not willing to be yourself around him."

"Whatever, you don't even know me anymore." I rolled my eyes, starting to feel my cheeks get warm from the alcohol.

"When I saw you today at work, that's the Maura I know: cracking jokes, being a smart-ass, and then immediately switching to a fearless, compassionate human being able to calm down a kid who would've had the police called on him if he had encountered anyone else. Your amount of empathy and how you are able to use it continually leaves me in awe. I feel like Ethan doesn't know that side of you. When I see you with him, all I can think of is how you were at the end of our relationship. How being with me made you."

"Oh, and how was I at the end?" I challenged, even though I knew. I still wanted to hear what he was finally taking responsibility for.

"Doubtful that God or anyone could love you simply for being who you are, rather than what you did or didn't do."

He paused. I didn't say anything.

I still struggled with this concept, but I wasn't sure what I could do to really fix it...just one more thing to add to the list of things I needed to work on.

"The more I pulled away from you, the harder you tried to be religious; like if you said more rosaries, went to Mass more, went to adoration longer, it would make God love you more and then I would love you more."

He looked over at the group.

"All of these young adults are constantly talking about how they want to marry someone who is the embodiment of holiness and challenges them to be holier. But a relationship shouldn't be based on an obstacle course of religious practices and traditions."

"Well, I'm sorry you have those concerns about the Blessed Sacrament Young Adult Group." I took another drink. "But I don't think it has anything to do with me or Ethan. And really, Sean, don't you think that when you decided to become a priest, you forfeited the ability to talk about what makes a relationship successful?"

I should have walked back to the table. That would've been the perfect exit line. Unfortunately, he had hooked me and I stood there, waiting for his retort. I was confident it would be some sort of apology.

"You tell him the people you've voted for in the past?"

And this was why he had driven me crazy whenever we fought when we were dating. No matter how clever I thought I could be, he always had something smarter to say, and he always did it in a calm and collected way that irritated me even more. This instance was no exception. He'd brought up something he knew I always kept secret for fear of judgment from more conservative Catholics like Ethan. My expression gave me away. Once again, this would have been a good time to walk away. But I didn't. I blame the whiskey.

"You don't think I'm good enough for him, do you?" I blurted out the insecurity.

That thought had haunted me with every relationship since Sean. It didn't help that a previous, bitchy roommate had told me that there were rumbles amongst the group that Sean would've chosen to marry me over becoming a priest if I'd been more devout and pious. But who was I kidding? I might as well have started that rumor myself because it was what I'd believed five years ago and part of me still believed it now.

"It has nothing to do with good enough, Maura. I think you deserve to be with someone you can be yourself around."

"Yeah, another liberal-leaning, cafeteria Catholic who's too tainted by the secular world to grasp what being a real Catholic is all about. That's just what a hippy like me deserves, right?"

He took a sip of his beer. It registered that perhaps he was able to remain more collected during the conversation because he still had beer in his glass, whereas mine was almost empty. He looked me straight in the eyes. I had forgotten how blue his eyes were, seeing as how I had avoided looking directly into them ever since he had returned to Seattle.

"You deserve to be loved unconditionally without having to worry if that person is going to change his mind when you admit to seeing grey when it comes to religion or faith. And I could be wrong; maybe Ethan's the type who loves debating issues and hearing different perspectives like I did...but those conversations should never leave you feeling invalidated or unloved."

He stopped. I could tell he regretted how his discernment process had hurt me. He knew that our past and the fear that I would experience the same pain again was the exact reason why I had been holding back my thoughts and opinions from Ethan. I stayed silent.

"I just want you to be with someone who can truly appreciate and love you for having the ability to see the other perspective, and who is open to being lovingly challenged by you, rather than trying to change you into some limited view of what they think is holy...but what would I know about successful relationships? I'm just a priest."

He turned his attention to Ethan, who was walking towards us.

"Hey, Maura, are you almost done?" Ethan called attention to my empty glass.

I nodded, finding it difficult to speak after the day, the conversation, and the drink I'd just had.

"Forgive me, Ethan," Sean smiled, turning on his charm. "I got to see this girl in action today at her work and I was just raving to her about how talented she is when it comes to handling a crisis."

"Oh, you had an exciting day?" Ethan questioned with surprise.

Earlier I had told him my day was 'okay and uneventful' when he'd asked.

"She pretty much stopped a two-hundred-and-fifty-pound kid from beating me up."

I rolled my eyes. "He's exaggerating," I clarified.

"Even so, it's impressive how she knows exactly what people need to hear in the moment, you know?" It sounded like a harmless question, but I knew Sean was asking it because he sensed Ethan had no idea I possessed this quality.

"Well, she is just all around impressive; that's why I love her," Ethan said, revealing to Sean exactly how serious the relationship was.

"So, are you ready to go?" I turned to Ethan abruptly, already stepping away from Sean before Ethan could answer, grabbing his hand.

"Have a good night, you two," Sean said cheerfully as he waved. I let Ethan say our goodbyes for me.

I let go of Ethan's hand after we stepped outside. I crossed my arms around my body, attempting to get warm.

"You want my coat?" he asked, chivalrous as usual.

I shook my head and kept walking. When we reached his car, he held open the car door for me. I got in, Sean's words still lingering in my head. Ethan remained silent on the short ride to my apartment, not attempting to draw me out. He parked in front of my building and turned to me.

"Are you okay? Is something wrong?"

I hesitated, debating how much I should tell him.

Remember, Maura, he loves you. You shouldn't be afraid to share things with him...especially if you're trying to be more than eighty percent in love with him some day.

"Was work that bad?"

"No," I said quickly. "Well, it's just..." I tried to think of how to explain it to him. "Sometimes when I have rough days at work, it's kind of hard to sit and listen to other people talk about certain things." I realized how vague I was being and felt sorry for him having to make the attempt to decode it.

"Is this about your conversation with Father Sean? Did he say something that upset you?"

When did Sean say something that didn't upset me? But I kept that thought to myself.

"No... yes," I sighed.

I was annoyed with Sean for pointing out things that I knew were potential challenges in my relationship with Ethan. I was frustrated with myself for allowing Sean's words to bother me. I was upset and worried about the situation with Justin. And finally, I was annoyed with some of the ignorant information I had heard that night regarding health care.

I wasn't sure how to clarify what I was really upset about, because, truthfully, there were so many negative feelings floating around my head that it was difficult for me to pinpoint what was wrong. Ethan looked at me, waiting for an answer.

"I don't know how to explain it," I admitted, sounding defeated.

"That's fine," he assured me, holding my hand. "Is there anything I can do to make it better?" he offered, sounding genuine.

I looked at him, knowing it was a combination of his eyes, the whiskey, and wanting to prove Sean wrong that led me to be honest.

"Stay with me tonight," I answered seriously.

"What?" His confusion registered immediately.

"I don't want to be alone. I just want to fall asleep next to you," I continued to put myself out there.

I didn't think I was asking for anything unacceptable. Sometimes I just wanted to be held. It seemed like a normal thing to want from my boyfriend. I stared at him, waiting for a response. His look of uncertainty told me his answer before he said anything.

"Maura, I don't think that's the best idea."

"Why? I'm not going to have sex with you," I said with conviction. "Please, I just want to be with you."

He let go of my hand, confirming that my plea wasn't going to work.

"Even so, it would create scandal, for you and for us. And I don't want that."

"Who cares? Whose business is it what we do? All that matters is if we're honest with ourselves," I said, my tone raising slightly. This was probably the most passionate Ethan had ever seen me.

"Maura, it's my job to protect you, and I'm not going to stay with you tonight," he said, almost as if he were talking to a small child. "Trust me, tomorrow after you've had a good night's rest, you will thank me for making this choice for us."

I knew there was no point in trying to convince him anymore. He let a silence pass.

"Do you want me to walk you to your door?"

I took a deep breath, letting it resonate that I had told Ethan exactly what I wanted from him to make me feel better, and he wasn't willing to give it to me. I added anger and embarrassment to the list of emotions I was feeling.

"No, I'm fine," I managed to get out calmly. "Thanks for the ride." I let myself out without kissing him goodbye.

I wanted him to chase after me, grab me in his arms, and plead for me to forgive him. As I walked through the door to my building and heard his car drive away, it was very clear that the dramatic conclusion I envisioned would not be happening.

I understood that my request was a grey area. Sleeping next to someone wasn't a sin, but it opened the possibility for sinful behavior, i.e. sex before marriage. Acting in a way that led to the mere assumption that someone had acted unchaste was viewed by a lot of people in the young adult group as almost as bad, if not just as bad, as premarital sex. They would often reference the Bible when this was brought up in discussion. I didn't agree, so I never put forth the effort to remember their supporting evidence...something, somewhere in Mark...maybe. Too bad I was unable to recall any piece of scripture that tells you to mind your own damn business.

It wasn't like I made a habit of spending the night with boy-friends. Honestly, it was only with Sean a handful of times after falling asleep while watching a movie, or the one time I got my wisdom teeth out and he took care of me. It was so comforting to be held in someone's arms who loved me and who I loved back. It made perfect sense that that was what I needed and wanted that night from Ethan.

As I lay in bed, I kept replaying how Ethan had denied my request. How he had talked to me like I was proposing something that was harmful to both of us. I questioned whether something I had viewed as completely innocent was, in fact, sinful. I just couldn't see how it could be, given my intentions and knowing the type of guy Ethan was.

Did I have something to be ashamed of? Were there any circumstances, outside of being married, where Ethan would have honored my request? Like maybe if I was sick or if someone I knew had died? Something told me that the context wouldn't have mattered to him and he would have made the same decision.

I thought of all the ways he could have met me halfway. He could have offered to stay until I fell asleep or slept on the floor next to the bed. He could have offered to do something else, but instead he just told me no and left it at that. I realized that compromising, even when it came to someone he claimed to love, was not something that Ethan was willing to do.

THOMAS

I had to admit, I was excited to be at Safeco Field again to see the Mariners, even if I was going to the game with a priest.

"Hey, Thomas," Father Sean called my attention to him.

"Hey."

"Sorry I'm a little late. I took the light rail and got turned around."

"Aren't you from Seattle?"

"Heck no. Iowan, born and raised," he said proudly.

"The over the top friendliness is all making sense now," I replied.

"Exactly. Anyway, let's get in there. I think you're going to be pretty blown away by how great the seats are," he said excitedly before turning to walk towards the gate.

When we entered onto the first level, that was enough for me to be impressed. Then an usher led us down the aisle all the way to the fifth row behind home plate.

"Is it good to be Harold Warren, or what?"

I barely nodded my head, still in awe.

"I think I'm in the wrong profession."

"You're not the one who took a vow of poverty," he joked.

I sat down.

"I'm going to get some dogs before it gets too busy. You want?"

"Yeah, sure." I started to get up.

"It's fine, I got it." He motioned for me to sit back down. He walked away before I had a chance to argue.

I relaxed back into my seat and let him go. I proceeded to take a picture and send it to Michael, knowing he would share my excitement, and reveling in how jealous he would be.

After I texted Michael, without thinking too much about it, I sent the picture to Maura:

> My Saturday night is already better
> than yours.

Was it weird that I had just sent her a text gloating about my Saturday night? In the past, I had only texted her clear-cut questions, never anything random like that. I wondered if she would respond or if there would be nothing for the rest of the night. I should have thought about that before sending the text like an idiot...but I don't know why I was so concerned. The comment was no different than something I would have said to her in person.

My phone went off and I looked down to see Michael's response.

> Fuck you.

I let out a laugh. Father Sean returned with two hot dogs and two beers. He held out the carrier for me to grab my hot dog and cup of over-priced beer.

"Thanks." I reached for my wallet.

"Nah, man, it's cool," he waved off my offer to pay him back.

"Are you sure?" I asked with my hand still on my wallet, ready to reimburse him. I knew my mother would be seriously disappointed in me if I let a priest pay for my food. In fact, she would probably be highly embarrassed by the fact that I hadn't bought him dinner.

"Yeah, seriously, you can hit me back later. Honestly, you're doing me a favor. My only other options for people to bring were the other Blessed Sacrament priests, and they get so cranky after nine o'clock. Especially Father Bernard.".

"What about all those guys who go to church with Maura?"

"The guys in the young adult group?" he clarified.

I nodded, thinking any of them would jump at the opportunity to go to a game with him.

He gave me a look. "No, definitely not. I mean, don't get me wrong, they're fine guys, just not the type I want to go to a ballgame with."

He could tell I wasn't grasping what made me a better choice.

"I'm making the assumption that you don't really view me as a church authority or highly influential in your faith journey?"

I wondered if it was a trick question and didn't answer him.

"Anyway, sometimes it's nice to hang out with somebody who doesn't see me as their spiritual leader, and I can just relax and be normal. Well, as normal as a priest can be," he joked. "Outside of the priory, I don't get much opportunity because they recommend you only let down around family and close friends who knew you before you took your vows," he explained. "But all of those people are in Iowa – besides Maura, who pretty much wants to slap me anytime she sees me, naturally."

I laughed. He wasn't as clueless about Maura as I had thought.

"Anyway, I appreciate having someone to go to the game with."

There was a pause in conversation as we started to eat. I was taking in what Father Sean had just shared. I had never thought about the social drawbacks of being a priest, other than the obvious one of not having sex.

"So, is Michael your only brother?"

I wasn't surprised that Father Sean was not the type to let a lull in conversation last too long. It was funny how much he and Maura had in common. I finished chewing.

"Yeah, but I have an older sister, too. I just texted Michael the view from our seats. He's pretty pissed off," I informed him proudly.

"That's cold-hearted," Father Sean reflected. "Remind me to send one to my brother," he added. "Did you play ball?"

"In high school. Mostly outfield, sometimes second base."

"I've been playing in this beer league with some of the grad students who go to Newman and their friends. We need another player. You interested? We play Thursdays at six in Ravenna Park."

The idea of getting to play baseball again was intriguing, but then again, I pictured having to play with a bunch of guys like Ethan. That was less than appealing. Father Sean sensed my hesitation.

"I promise we just play and grab a beer afterwards. Four guys on the team aren't even Catholic."

"Thursdays?"

He nodded.

"Sure, why not?" I figured I could always come up with some excuse to quit if it turned out to be weird.

Within minutes, they had us standing for the National Anthem and the game was underway. Father Sean followed the unwritten rules of going to a baseball game with another guy, meaning he didn't talk very much and when he did, it had to do with the game. I appreciated that.

In the bottom of the second, Cano hit a home run into right field, bringing in one additional run. The stadium went wild. When things calmed down, Father Sean turned to me.

"Last time I was here, like five years ago, Griffey was back, and I was in that same section with Maura. Bottom of the seventh, Mariners down by one against the A's, and Griffey just smashes one out there. So textbook, so beautiful. It heads right for us and I catch it. Probably one of the manliest moments I've ever had in my life. I give Maura the ball, thinking I'm the most amazing guy ever," he paused, holding my attention with his story, "and within two minutes she ended up giving it to some seven-year-old boy a couple seats down from us." He shook his head, disappointment showing on his face. "And that's the real reason we broke up," he said in a serious tone but then quickly smiled. "Man, I was so pissed...scratch that, I'm still pissed...I totally would've asked for the ball back in the breakup if she hadn't been so altruistic and given it away. I mean, seriously, Ken Griffey Jr!" he lamented.

"I'm surprised you're still willing to talk to her," I said, thinking how upset I would've been had that happened to me five years ago. In fact, I didn't think I would've given the ball to any woman I'd ever dated to start with. I wondered what that said about me.

At that moment, my phone went off. Maura had responded.

> I don't know -- I AM watching Seven
> Brides for Seven Brothers with my
> mom tonight. It's a tie.

> Bless your beautiful hide.

I referenced...teased...flirted...shit, it was getting harder to tell.

Her response was cleverer than I expected.

> It's a good thing you're in a place
> that has an excess of balls...you seem
> to have lost yours.

I was unable to keep from laughing, which got Father Sean's attention.

"Your brother going off about the seats again?" He looked over briefly at me before looking back at the game.

"Uh, no, it was just Maura."

In any other circumstance it would've been weird admitting that I was talking to his ex-girlfriend. But since he had decided to become a priest, I felt like the normal rules of territory didn't apply... not that I was even interested in her in that way. She was just a friend.

"Huh," he reflected, mimicking my nonchalant tone. He paused while Hernandez made the third out, then turned back to me while the Red Sox took the field. "You two talk a lot?"

"Not really. You know Maura; she's friendly with everybody."

"True," he agreed, neither of us facing one another now, our eyes on the batter. After Seager got on first, I took the opportunity to respond to Maura.

```
I worry that if I got any balls
here, you would end up giving them
away to the first kid who asked
for them.


Tell Sean to get over it,
```

she fired back her response.

I smiled, imagining the expression I knew she would have had when she responded.

Father Sean looked over at me with a knowing smile.

"What? She's funny sometimes." I justified.

"She is," he agreed.

We went back to watching the game, but I knew he was going to bring her up again.

"So, what's the deal with you guys? Are you interested in her?"

I hadn't expected him to flat out ask me that.

"Uh, no," I said simply. "She's not really my type, and clearly, I'm not her type; see current and previous guys she's dated."

"I'm getting lumped in with Ethan?" he said with feigned offense.

I shrugged, not denying the comparison.

"I like to think I have a little more personality than him."

His openness surprised me.

"So then are you looking for someone?" he asked.

I raised an eyebrow at him. "To date?"

He nodded.

"Not really. You recruiting me for the priesthood right now?" I pushed back.

"Ha, yeah right," he grinned. "I'm not saying it could never happen, Thomas, but I think you would need to come to church a little more often before the Dominicans started vetting you. No offense."

"None taken."

"I'm just offering to wingman. In a morally appropriate manner, of course."

"Wow, that's an interesting take on wing-manning if I ever heard one," I replied unenthusiastically.

He could tell I doubted his ability.

"On your three o'clock there're two brunettes who keep looking over here at us," he said nonchalantly, proving his skill while maintaining his stare at the field.

I casually looked over and caught the eye of one of them, who smiled shyly at me before looking away and then giggling to her friend who not so casually turned her head and smiled directly at me, raising her cup to me. They looked to be about my age and were both attractive. Not wanting to be rude, I smiled and mimicked the gesture before taking a drink and then looked back at the game.

"I'm impressed you picked up on that," I admitted.

"I'm celibate, not blind."

We paused to watch Cano again, hoping it would lead to a run. It ended up being a fly ball sent to right and caught.

"So are you going to go talk to them?" he encouraged.

"And say what? My priest friend and I want to buy you a drink after the game?" I scoffed.

"You don't have to tell them I'm a priest."

"You telling me to lie, Father?"

He looked at me with frustration. I humored him briefly.

"So, let's say we go out with them after the game. Then what? You're not going to want me to go home with either of them. What's the point?"

"You don't know, you might end up really liking one of them and may decide to take her out on an actual date."

"That's cute," I made light of his suggestion. My phone vibrated with another text from Maura. "But no thanks," I said before reading her text.

```
If you can name all seven brothers
without looking it up, I'll give you
a prize.
```

Maybe I was reading too much into it, but it seemed like she was flirting with me, in her own innocent Maura way. There was no way she would ever know if I looked it up or not, but I played fair. I began entering the names: Adam, Benjamin, Caleb, Daniel, Frank...

"You wouldn't happen to know the E and G names of the brothers from Seven Brides for Seven Brothers, would you?" I asked Father Sean.

He raised an eyebrow at me.

"Maura says she'll give me a prize if I can name all seven," I explained with amusement.

"You ever think there might be another reason why you're not interested in talking to those girls?" Father Sean called me back into the conversation.

"Seriously? We just went over this. She's a non-factor. I mean, unless the prize ends up being meaningless sex," I joked.

I figured the off-color joke would make him want to protect Maura from me and move on from the subject. His expression told me that I was walking a thin line, which was the reaction I had intended.

"Ephraim and Gideon," I declared aloud when the memory clicked. I couldn't believe I remembered all seven without help.

```
Adam, Benjamin, Caleb, Daniel,
Frank, Ephraim, Gideon.
```

Impulsively, I sent another text.

```
What's my prize? It better be sexy.
```

I sent it purely because I knew it would fluster her. I returned to the conversation.

"You know you don't want riff-raff like me interested in her anyway," I argued.

"Fair enough," he granted, and let it drop.

The game ended up being fairly exciting. The Red Sox tied it up in the seventh inning. I had stopped checking my phone for Maura's response because the game was too interesting. The Mariners were down by one at the end of the eighth. Cruz ended the game in the bottom of the ninth with a walk off home run. Father Sean and I celebrated along with everyone around us as we watched the team gathering around Cruz when he reached home plate.

"Yes!" Father Sean exclaimed, clapping his hands together and smiling. "So glad they didn't lose!"

He spoke like a true Mariner fan.

"You want to grab a beer?" Father Sean suggested as we headed out of the stadium.

"Sure."

It was still surreal that hanging out with him one-on-one hadn't been awkward. We found our way to a bar down the street, busy with other fans who'd had the same postgame idea as us. We were able to find a high-top cocktail table in the corner before the place became standing room only.

An attractive blonde waitress waited on us. She seemed quite taken with Father Sean, asking him questions about the game, touching his arm, laughing at his responses. After she had served us our drinks and was out of earshot, I finally asked the question I had been trying to fathom ever since I'd ever known about celibacy and the priesthood.

"So that doesn't bother you?"

"What?"

I couldn't tell if he was feigning cluelessness.

"The waitress clearly hitting on you. It doesn't bother you when women do that?"

"Oh, here we go," he grinned. "It's the sex question. Frankly, Thomas, I expected you to hold out a little longer before asking," he teased.

"Sorry," I apologized half-heartedly but I still wanted an explanation.

"Nah, it's fine. I've been hanging out with so many devout people who act like it's not weird, that I haven't been asked in a while."

He paused.

"So what do you want to know?" he threw it back to me.

I wasn't sure where to start.

"How?"

"How what?"

If I was going to be nosy, he was going to make me work for it.

"How can you not?"

Considering how good-looking the waitress was, I knew if she had flirted with me like she had with him, I would've happily taken her home with me, given the chance.

"Let me ask you this," he started, "when was the last time you had sex?"

I paused trying to think of when Natalie had left for Spring break.

"A little over a month ago."

"Okay, fair enough. And have you thought about sex since then?"

I wondered if this was a trap and he was somehow tricking me into saying a confession without being at church.

"Yes," I said hesitantly.

"Did it prevent you from being able to function in your every-day life?"

"No, but it's only been a little over a month, not..."

"Six years," he filled in the timeline for me.

I let out a heavy sigh thinking how hard six years without sex would be.

"No one ever died from not having sex. Our ability to exercise self-control is what separates us from animals. I'm not saying there aren't days when I think about it or want it. Of course, that's natural. But I made the choice to commit to something else, and it doesn't kill me to abstain. I imagine it's like giving up smoking; you're always going to want a cigarette, but after a while, it just becomes more of a habit not to smoke, and you don't put yourself in situations where you're more likely to engage in the habit."

"So no strip club after this?" I joked.

"From what I remember, the strippers aren't allowed to have sex with you," he quipped back, letting me know he wasn't as inno-cent as I thought he was.

"So, just so we're clear...you have had..." I paused.

"Sex?" he laughed. "Really, Thomas, you going prude on me now? Yes, I have gotten laid before. Probably too much for my own good."

"So why give it up?"

"Because I wanted to be a priest more than I wanted to get married and have sex," he said simply.

"Once again, so I'm clear, you have had sex before? Are you sure you weren't just having really bad sex?"

He shook his head and looked amused at my inability to grasp the possibility of wanting something more than sex.

"Man, I don't know how else to explain it to you. I know it doesn't make sense to most, but that's just how it is."

"I mean, it would make more sense to me if you had never done it, or like, if you were really awkward or bad-looking...but..." I sighed, unable to finish my point, so instead I took a drink of beer. "I mean, was Maura that bad of a girlfriend?"

He laughed.

"No, honestly she was probably the best girlfriend I ever had," Father Sean reflected. "We bickered a lot, but I could've easily married her."

"Then why?"

He shrugged, knowing once again it wasn't going to make sense to me.

"After making many poor decisions at Notre Dame and a few years after college, I came back to the Church when my dad was diagnosed with cancer and died four months later. By the time I moved to Seattle for grad school, the priesthood had crossed my mind more than a few times, which I shook off as completely unrealistic, given my past. I didn't think I was capable of it. And then I met Maura. Being with her just made me..." He paused, looking unsure how to continue. "It's hard to explain without sounding cheesy, but she just has a way of making people realize how unconditional and compassionate God's love is for them. It's like she looks at people and only sees potential."

I let his words sink in, considering whether she'd had that effect on me.

"Isn't that exactly the type of woman guys like you want to marry?" I challenged, thinking I was owed an explanation for her sake.

He took a drink and nodded as he swallowed, appearing to have thought over the question many times before.

"I know, I know," he admitted. "Like I said, it doesn't make sense."

He paused.

"Man, I got so close to buying a ring, putting a down payment on a house; but when I thought about marrying her, the parts I was most excited about had nothing to do with her. It was all about how much service we were going to do together. And I started noticing that the time I felt most complete and the most at peace weren't the times when I was with her. It was at church, by myself. Yeah, it's good to have a strong personal faith, but not to the point where your spouse becomes a complete afterthought. It wouldn't have been fair to her," he confessed.

"The unfortunate thing is that Maura is so loving and loyal that she probably would have let me be a shitty, distracted husband, just as she let me be a shitty, distracted boyfriend for the last half of our relationship. Thankfully, I had just enough sense of selfless-ness to know that my own fears and reservations about being a priest weren't enough let her end up in a crappy marriage that she didn't deserve."

It still didn't make sense to me, but I doubted he would be able to explain it more sufficiently.

After a moment passed he said, "What can I say? Sometimes you don't know what you need or want until you're brave enough to honestly consider a possibility that terrifies you."

His statement resonated with me. I wasn't sure why. Potentially, it was the amount of conviction he'd said it with. We went back to drinking our beers and watching the highlights of the game being played on the TVs above the bar. The bar gradually got louder and busier. It was a rare night when both the Sounders and the Mariners had played at home, which explained the crowd.

"Shop Boy!" I heard someone call in our direction.

I didn't think it was directed at me, until I felt a tap on my shoulder. I turned around to see the intern from Maura's work, Ashland, standing in front of me. She was wearing a Sounders T-shirt, which she had tied in the back so that it fit more tightly in the front. Her navel piercing was revealed by her low-cut jeans. I noticed for the first time the stud in her nose. Her long dark hair was up in a ponytail.

"Thomas!" she exclaimed.

"Hello," I said politely but with less enthusiasm.

"What're you doing here?" she demanded.

"Just grabbing a beer after the Mariners game." I lifted my glass to show her. "You?"

"The Sounders won, so we thought we'd come celebrate," she yelled over the noise, putting her drink down on our table. She rested her hand on my shoulder, moving her face close to mine to talk into my ear.

"I saw you when we walked in, and my friends totally dared me to come talk to you," she giggled as she stepped back.

Ashland was clearly tipsy, if not drunk. I was surprised by her overt friendliness, because she had never said much to me before. Then again, there had been a couple of times when I'd caught her checking me out at the youth center.

"Hi, I'm Ashland," she exclaimed, holding out her hand to Father Sean.

"Sean," he shook her hand. He left his title off.

"You look familiar," she said, squinting, trying to place his face.

"He volunteers at the youth center, too. Ashland is the graduate intern at the center," I explained to Father Sean.

She continued to stare at him. Then her eyes grew wide in revelation. "Oh my God! You're the priest!" she exclaimed loudly, taking a step into me and leaning against my arm.

Father Sean just nodded.

"Wait, you're allowed to go to bars?" she asked naively. She turned to me. "That's crazy," she proclaimed, looking for my agreement.

I made eye contact with Father Sean, confirming that he also thought she was a little out of it.

"Yep, it is pretty crazy," I agreed with her, unable to keep from smiling.

"So, Mr. Man-chanic, are you like, religious, too?" she asked disdainfully.

"Not particularly," I was honest. I was certain this would not be new or upsetting information to Father Sean.

She took another drink.

"Did you just call me 'Man-chanic'?" I laughed.

"That's what I call you behind your back, because you're hot," she confessed freely.

"I guess it's better than 'Grease Monkey.'"

"And I call you Father What-A-Waste," she said looking over at Father Sean. "No offense, but you're like, way hotter without the dress," she referenced his Dominican robes that he was not wearing.

He smiled, more amused by her inebriated state than offended.

"I totally was going to try and hook my friend up with you before I knew who you were."

She pointed to the corner at a group of young people in Sounders gear. The woman she looked to be pointing at was making out with a guy.

"It looks like your friend already found someone to hook up with. God must've been looking out for her," Father Sean reflected dryly.

It was funny to see Ashland trying to figure out how serious he was.

"Whelp, I better get going before I get in trouble with the Archbishop. He sometimes does sweeps of the bars on Saturday nights," Father Sean continued his sarcasm. "Wouldn't want the Pope to find out I've been having fun. You know how it goes," he sighed.

He stepped over to me while Ashland was distracted by her drink. He knew a good wingman never lingered longer than needed.

"I'm trusting that you will make gentlemanly choices," he said, grabbing my shoulder firmly. I assured him with a nod.

"Thanks for the beer. I'll see you at Ravenna on Thursday. Have a good night." He eyed me severely, further communicated his expectations that I not take advantage of Ashland.

"Ashland, good to officially meet you." He shook her hand before leaving us alone.

"So, you're a Sounders fan?"

"Um, yes, clearly," she said emphatically. "It's a superior sport to boring old baseball, obviously."

I dramatically dropped my mouth open.

"How can you say that, Ashland? Baseball is America's pastime. Soccer is for communists. Then again, aren't you studying social work? That would make sense," I joked.

"Pfft, baseball is for pussies," she exclaimed. "No offense."

She seemed to think that phrase would allow her to get away with saying anything she wanted. She took another sip of her drink.

"How about you tell me exactly why soccer is better than baseball?" I invited.

"It's fast and it's rough." She raised an eyebrow at me, driving home her innuendo.

"That must be why I like baseball. I think scoring is a lot more satisfying when you can take your time." I held eye contact with her for a moment, showing that I also could make innuendos.

I glanced over at the corner and no longer saw her group. "Are your friends still here?" She looked over and then started scanning the whole bar.

"I don't see them." She pulled out her phone and proceeded to make a call. No one answered so she tried sending a text. She was a little more uncoordinated than I'd originally noticed, swaying slightly as she focused on her phone.

Ashland looked at me and grinned. "I think they left me."

"Those soccer fans can be such hooligans."

"Oh!" she exclaimed when her phone lit up with a text. "Okay, they just went down the street to a different bar," she explained. "How about you come with me?" She grabbed my hand and started to pull me towards the door.

I couldn't deny I was enjoying her attention, but I thought of Father Sean's parting words and the fact that I would see her every Wednesday for the next few weeks regardless of how the night ended. If this had been a few months ago, I probably would've made an entirely different decision.

"Tell you what, I will walk you there, but I'm going to head home after that."

I walked her out of the crowded bar.

"No," she stated disappointedly. "You should come. It'll be so much more fun if you're there."

She wrapped both of her hands around mine.

"It's just two doors down." She led me that direction. I think she thought that my following meant I was conceding to her request rather than just ensuring she got there safely. When we arrived, I stopped following her and let go of her hand.

"Well, have a good rest of the night, Ashland."

She let out a dramatic sigh. "Come on, it's way too early to go home."

"Maybe for Sounders fans, but us baseball pussies like to turn in early."

She didn't seem to appreciate my humor and put her lips in a pout. When it was clear that I wasn't going to be swayed, she switched her tactic from childish pout to sexy seduction, sliding her eyes up and down my body in an unmistakable come-on. She stepped in close, placing her hands on my chest.

"Is there anything I can do to convince you to stay?"

I took a deep breath and let it out, almost about to waver. "You should probably get in there before your friends ditch you again," I reminded her.

She continued to press herself against me. "I'm not going in until you kiss me," she declared.

I raised my brow at her, feeling like she had backed me into a corner. I considered my options. One, push her away and potentially insult her. Two, wait her out and continue to stand there awkwardly with a drunk girl pressed up against me outside of a bar. Three, kiss her and get her to go inside the bar.

I took too long to decide, because before I knew it, Ashland's lips were on mine. I tried to hold back, but well, she was hot. I slipped my tongue in her mouth. She broke away.

"Good night, Thomas."

She gave me a small smile and walked away, no longer extending the invitation for me to join her.

I was thankful she didn't ask me again, because I knew I was weak and would've given in to just about anything after that kiss. I willed myself to begin the walk back to my truck. I checked my phone to distract myself. There was a response from Maura sent over three hours earlier.

Sexy prizes are my specialty.

Well that caught me off guard. After giving it some thought, I started to doubt whether Maura had actually sent it. There was no way she had it in her to type something like that, especially to someone like me...when she had a boyfriend like Ethan. I had to be reading too much into it. She probably meant for it to be sarcastic. I had successfully distracted myself from Ashland but I was now thinking about Maura...and not in a way I should've been thinking about her.

Driving home, I tried to keep my mind off both women by thinking about baseball. It was futile. My brain kept returning to Ashland's kiss...her navel ring...her ass in those jeans. Why didn't the moral victory of not taking advantage of her feel more fulfilling?

MAURA

After how we ended things on Wednesday, I remained frustrated with Ethan for the rest of the week. Had he been right to tell me no? I had started to question my morality, which was a first. I didn't want to see him for Adoration that Friday, but not going would just be another strike against me in his eyes. I sought solace in the fact that Adoration didn't require any talking. I wasn't so irritated that I couldn't sit next to him and pray in silence for an hour or two. Who knew? Maybe praying would make me less upset about the whole situation.

It didn't.

"You want to go grab some ice cream or something?" Ethan asked as we walked to his car afterwards.

"I'm not really hungry."

It was the truth. Guilt was the best appetite suppressant. We drove back to my apartment in silence. Once we parked, the silence continued.

"So, are we going to talk about Wednesday?" he started the conversation. "I feel like you're mad at me, even though I didn't do anything wrong."

This was a bold way to start off reconciling with a girlfriend. I didn't say anything. I didn't want to agree with him, but I didn't think

I could stand my ground arguing that I was justified in being mad at him.

"Maura, I love you. What I said from the beginning about not wanting to make any mistakes is true. I'm not going to put myself in a situation where I'm tempted to act unchaste. I figured most women would appreciate that respect."

I didn't respond.

"Do you not?"

"No," I sighed, "I mean, yes, I do appreciate it, but..." I stopped, not knowing what else to say. Telling him it was important for me to fall asleep next to him before we were married seemed trivial now.

"I just don't think you understand how hard it is for a guy to hold back in certain situations. And I've never dated anyone who's asked me to compromise like you did on Wednesday night."

"I'm sorry," I said reflexively, but I wasn't sure if I was or even should be sorry.

"It's fine, I believe you had pure intentions," he assured me. "I just want to make sure we're on the same page before we move forward."

He looked at me expectantly. I found myself nodding. I mean, I had never had anyone take a stand to protect my chastity before. Wasn't I supposed to want that?

"So, no more requests for sleepovers?" he verified.

I nodded again.

He took my hand. "You know, if you weren't so beautiful, none of this would be a problem."

I gave him a small smile.

"Can I take you out tomorrow?" he asked.

"I told my mom I would spend the weekend with her." I was relieved we would have a little bit of a break, a chance to reset from this whole experience.

"You know, I would love to spend more time getting to know your parents," he cajoled, fishing for an invite.

"You've met my parents."

"Just at Mass. That doesn't give me much opportunity to gather embarrassing stories about you as a child," he reasoned.

"Well, my dad is on a fishing trip this weekend, so it's strictly a mother-daughter day," I explained. "You can come to dinner with us in a couple weeks for my birthday," I offered.

"That's right, your birthday is coming up," he reflected. "Have you thought about what you want?"

"No, not really." I never expected anything from anyone beyond wishing me a happy birthday.

"Hmmm, interesting." He sounded like he doubted me. "Good thing I've already gotten your present," he said enticingly.

"Well, are you going to give me any clues?" I was not above ruthlessly trying to guess surprises before they were revealed.

"Um," he pretended to think, "no."

"Come on, you can't tell me you have it two weeks ahead of time and then not offer any clues." This was sound logic to me.

"Why yes, I believe I can," he countered playfully.

If it had been a week ago, I would have kissed him. But now I worried he would judge me for using physical affection to persuade him. I resorted to staring him down.

"Let's just say you'll be pleasantly surprised," he offered vaguely, leaning in to kiss me goodnight. I was relieved that the kiss wasn't as reserved as when we'd first started dating. I felt my shoulders relax for the first time all night and had a genuine smile on my face when he broke away.

* * *

Despite having to answer a barrage of questions about Ethan from my mother — the most annoying being whether I thought he was "the one" — I was genuinely happy to spend my Saturday with her. It had been a while since we'd had a full day to ourselves. We filled it with shopping and getting pedicures. After feeling like a subpar girlfriend and Christian for the last few days, it was nice to be around somebody who loved me unconditionally.

My mom absolutely hated it when my dad spent the night away, so it was no surprise when she suggested that I spend the night at home. Normally, I would've argued that that was silly because I was a grown-up now, but I knew I needed mothering just as much as she needed the company.

"I bought your favorite ice cream and already put some sparkling wine in the refrigerator," she exclaimed once we got back to the house. As always, she had been expecting me.

"What should we watch tonight?"

I shrugged, not feeling particularly picky because no matter what we watched, I'd be eating ice cream.

"Oh, I know! Daddy got me Seven Brides for Seven Brothers for our anniversary and I haven't been able to watch it yet."

This was what I got for letting her pick. It was unfair to complain now. Don't get me wrong, I like musicals, I just was not a fan of that one in particular. It must have been that it was basically an ad in favor of Stockholm syndrome. Who cares if a man kidnaps you? As long as he puts a ring on it, everything's peachy.

"Sounds good," I smiled for her benefit.

We settled in on the couch with our ice cream and sparkling wine. I tried to estimate how long it would take before we both fell asleep. I checked the time on my phone and saw a text from Thomas.

It was odd that he would text me on a Saturday night, especially since I had consistently been turning down his offers to hang out. He had sent a picture of his seats at the Mariners game with a message gloating about how close to home plate he was. I sent him a sarcastic response about *Seven Brides for Seven Brothers* being equally awesome.

"Who's that? Is it Ethan?" my mother asked excitedly.

"Uh, no, it's just Thomas." I put my phone back down. I should have lied and said it was Sydney.

"O'Hollaren?" Her expression confirmed I should have followed my instinct and lied.

"Yeah, he's just gloating about having good seats at the Mariners game." I hoped that my nonchalant tone would calm her down.

"I'm so glad you guys finally became friends," she reflected. "Jackie thinks you've been such a good influence on him. I think she's a little disappointed you have a boyfriend."

"Even if I were single, I'm not really his type. It wouldn't work out," I attempted to squash any possible fantasies that were formulating in her head, knowing that for years she had hoped somehow I would magically end up with one of her friends' sons.

"What? He doesn't like smart, talented, beautiful, caring girls?" my mom asked defensively.

I sighed, thinking I had met my quota of girl talk with her for the day, possibly the week.

"Mom, he's not religious."

"Oh, nonsense, I see him with Jackie at church all the time."

I raised my eyebrows in surprise. I thought he had only been to Mass with his family the one time on Easter. But I had to consider the source. To my mom, 'all the time,' probably meant that she had seen him, or even someone that looked like him, like twice.

"Maybe if you went to the 9 a.m. Mass with your dad and me more you would know that," she said.

I disregarded her attempted to guilt me and went back to my phone. Thomas had made a reference about the movie. I quipped back about his manliness. My mom was eagerly waiting for an update on the conversation.

"I thought we were watching the movie?" I asked before she could get another question in. My mother gave me a look of inspection and then turned her attention back to the movie.

More entertained by Thomas than the movie, I challenged him to name all seven brothers, offering a prize if he did it correctly. I was curious just how extensive his family-friendly film knowledge was. He responded relatively quickly with all seven names. No doubt he looked them all up. It didn't surprise me when he demanded that his prize be sexy.

I had known Thomas long enough to know that he had specifically done that to make me uncomfortable and poke fun at me. Impulsively, I decided I would give him a taste of his own medicine. I sent back a flirty response, saying that sexy prizes were my specialty. I thought he would joke back.

Five minutes passed without a response...followed by fifteen... followed by two hours. *Shit. Shit. Shiiiiiit.* What had I been thinking texting something like that to him? At the end of the night, I found myself lying in my childhood bedroom unable to sleep because he had never responded, and my head was filled with all the horrible possibilities of what he was thinking about that stupid text I'd sent.

Ugh. The worst part was that I didn't even have alcohol to blame. I glanced at the clock to see that it was after one in the morning. I tried to convince myself that Thomas had probably fallen asleep long ago and I was the last thing on his mind...or more likely he was awake, fooling around with some woman he'd met at a bar...either way, I had to be the last thing on his mind.

Unfortunately, this rationalization led to me picturing Thomas making out with someone. Someone tall and skinny with blonde hair, probably wearing a halter top. I bet she had a name like Alexis or Arianna. I tried to stop picturing the scene, but I just couldn't get it out of my head. Eventually I started thinking about what his kiss would feel like...what sort of things he would say to me. I tried to get myself to stop, even resorting to replaying memories of making out with Sean, but it was no use.

A normal person would've been thinking about her own boyfriend, but now it seemed so inappropriate to even picture making out with Ethan. More awkward than anything.

Great. I would rather fantasize about pretty much anyone else over my own boyfriend? That sounds healthy.

Damn it, this was Sean's fault for making me doubt how I felt. Or maybe it was Ethan's for being so orthodox. Really it was my fault for not being attracted to what was best for me.

My alarm went off at eight and I regretted the decision to appease my mom by spending the night and going to nine a.m. Mass with her. I tried my best to put myself together and cover the large circles under my eyes, the visible result of my neuroticism that had lasted until well after three a.m.

"Good morning, Sweetie," my mom exclaimed enthusiastically as she reached to take a sip of coffee.

I felt hungover, minus the excruciating headache, thank God. I mumbled good morning and poured myself a glass of water.

"I really like that top," my mom complimented.

"Thank you," I responded quietly.

She looked at me with concern.

"Maurie, are you okay? Did you not sleep well?"

Predictably, she walked over and felt my forehead like I was a child. I considered feigning sickness to get out of Mass for fear that Thomas was going to be there, but knew that if I did, my mother would insist on waiting on me hand and foot. I had enough of a moral compass to know that it would be wrong to make her do that just because I was an idiot.

"No, I'm fine," I smiled. "I guess it's just hard to get used to a different bed." I finished my water. "Ready to go?" I tried to mirror her exuberance.

She nodded and we headed out the door.

Ethan was standing outside the front entrance of the church waiting for us. This was unexpected, but yesterday he had asked what Mass I was going to. I saw my mom's face fill with delight.

"Well, what a pleasant surprise," she greeted him.

He was wearing a suit and tie. It had been a while since I had seen him in his fancy Mass attire. Then I realized it was Pentecost, the birthday of the Church. Of course Ethan would wear a suit. And now I felt underdressed, despite wearing one of my nicer shirts.

"Good to see you again, Mrs. McCormick." He shook her hand.

"Oh, please, call me Laura," she insisted before she went in to hug him.

"You look surprised to see me," Ethan commented, giving me a quick side hug.

"I just didn't think you'd want to come to the early Mass," I explained.

"Who else would I want to celebrate Pentecost with?"

It amused me that he referred to Pentecost as something to be observed like a holiday. I mean, technically, it was a holiday, but not one that people did anything to celebrate outside of going to church...at least I didn't think anyone did. Was he being clever? Maybe he'd grown up celebrating Pentecost with his family.

I pictured him and all of his family sitting around a table eating a formal dinner, the room decorated in red. Yep, that seemed to be the only type of fantasy I could muster when thinking of Ethan: celebrating random Catholic holidays. Was that normal or weird? At least I wasn't objectifying him.

We took our seats on the right side of the church, near the statue of Saint Catherine of Siena. This was Ethan's favorite place to sit, not just because it was near Saint Catherine, but because it was towards the front. Ethan never sat more than six rows back. He said he liked how it made Mass feel more intimate. I asked him one time why he didn't just go to a smaller church. He said smaller parishes were never able to replicate the holiness he felt in a church like Blessed Sacrament. Must've been all the stained glass and brick.

I waited to see how my mom would react to being pulled out of her comfort zone as a chronic middle pew dweller. She continued to smile. Being at Mass with Ethan seemed to be enough to weather any change in habit. We knelt down to prepare for Mass. Ethan, of course, looked the most reverent of the three of us, resting his head against his folded hands, his eyes closed. Typically, I mimicked his body language, but today I stared straight ahead at the altar, zoning out due to my lack of sleep. Then, just as it had happened at Easter, I saw the Michael O'Hollaren clan file in.

I realized we were sitting in their typical area and my heart started to race when I saw Jackie walk in behind Michael's family. They sat one row directly behind us. Jackie said a quiet hello to my mother. A few moments passed and I thought I had avoided having to see Thomas.

I was just about to let out a mental sigh of relief when I saw Margaret's family walk in, Thomas included. He was holding Margaret's oldest daughter, making him look more appealing as a human, unfortunately. He caught my stare before I could look away. Good thing Ethan's eyes were still closed because he gave me a cocky smirk. I felt my lips reflexively purse. He was probably thinking of a million ways to make fun of me for that stupid text. Before walking past, he winked at me. My visible annoyance only seemed to amuse him more.

At least we were in front of the O'Hollarens. It made it easier to pretend like Thomas wasn't there. That is, until the sign of peace. My mother was all over the place, treating it like social hour with Jackie and her family. After Ethan had kissed me on the forehead like he usually did, I decided not turning around to exchange the sign of peace with someone I knew would look suspicious. I turned around to see Thomas, staring directly into my eyes.

"Peace be with you."

I held out my hand and shook his quickly before letting go and turning to his sister Margaret and her husband. I think I managed to look natural. I turned back around and grabbed Ethan's hand, counting the seconds until the next part of Mass.

Is this what those people who get caught cheating feel like? Wait. Did I cheat?

I didn't think I had. Then again, in Ethan's eyes, I had questionable morals when it came to napping with people. What was I going to do if Thomas decided to be funny and bring up that stupid text? The thought of trying to explain to Ethan how I thought I was being clever put a knot in my stomach. He rarely understood when I was trying to be clever to begin with. *God, I was stupid.*

Communion took forever and Father Jack made sure the conclusion of Mass would never end. The fate of my relationship with Ethan was dependent upon whether Thomas decided to be a smartass about my indiscretion. Maybe I was being dramatic, but I didn't want to take my chances. I ushered Ethan out of the pew towards the side exit as quickly as I could, ditching my mom because I knew she was going to stop and talk to Jackie.

Ethan turned to me when we were outside.

"Where'd your mom go?" He looked around.

"Oh, I thought she was right behind us," I lied. "She must have stopped to talk to the O'Hollarens."

"You didn't want to stay behind to talk to them, too?"

"No. Why?" I made my best attempt to sound casual.

Ethan gave me a half smile. "Maura, I never said you had to be cold to him. Do you want to go back in there and say hi?"

"No, I'd rather find out what you did last night without me around to entertain you." I straightened his tie as I changed the subject.

"Nothing much. I mostly read."

"And here I thought you would be writing sonnets about me," I said sarcastically.

"Sorry, I've never really been the creative type," he said unapologetically, but took my hand.

"It's okay," I sighed. "I guess it's a flaw I can overlook."

I made him smile. The knot in my stomach started to loosen.

"Oh, well, how kind of you." He kissed me on the cheek before he pulled out his phone.

Good. I was back on track.

"I have six missed calls from my boss," he announced. "Would you excuse me for a second?"

He let go of my hand and walked away as he made a call. I commanded myself not to analyze how formal he still was with me. He was a gentleman...and I needed to get it together before I blew it. I said hello to a few of my parents' friends while waiting on the sidewalk for my mother.

"I have to say I am thoroughly impressed by the efficiency with which you rush out of Mass when you're here." I heard Thomas' voice behind me.

There was that knot again.

I turned around and hated that I noticed that he'd gotten a haircut. I hated even more that I thought it looked good.

"Good morning, Thomas," I said evenly with my arms crossed. "I'm surprised to see you here this morning; I would've guessed you'd be hung over."

"Me too, but Father Sean is apparently the type who likes to turn in early. He had some sort of Sunday morning obligation."

I looked over to see if Ethan was done with his phone call. Thomas noticed I was distracted and called my attention back to him.

"I finally met your mother."

I nodded.

"She said she's going to invite me to be her friend on this new thing she just joined called 'Facebook.'"

"Did she?" My eyes grew wide with embarrassment.

"No, she didn't, but now I think I'm going to have to make that happen. She said she wants to help me find a girlfriend."

I sighed, knowing he wasn't joking about that.

"Sorry," I apologized for her. "She likes to be overly helpful."

"Gee, I don't know anyone like that," he reflected teasingly.

"Excuse me, I am the right amount of helpful," I defended, making him laugh.

Ethan joined us. He placed his hand on my lower back. Wow. This, on top of the kiss on my cheek, was significant post-Mass PDA for Ethan.

"Thomas, hello again," Ethan greeted, shaking Thomas' hand.

"Ethan," Thomas nodded.

"I hate to do this," Ethan turned to me, "but I actually have to head into work. They're having a huge problem with some of the code for a new program they wanted to launch this week."

I never would have thought a computer programmer could get called into work on an emergency. But whatever got him away from Thomas and the chance of finding out about that stupid text could only be a good thing for me.

Shit. That was a selfish thing to think.

"Say goodbye to your mother for me and tell her I look forward to seeing her next week for your birthday."

I nodded. He kissed my cheek.

"I love you. I'll call you tonight."

"Love you too." Why did it still not feel normal to say that?

"Good to see you again, Thomas. You should come out with us again sometime."

Ethan's invitation surprised me. He was probably trying to show me there was no need for me to be unfriendly toward Thomas. Thomas simply nodded, not verbally committing to anything.

"So, will you be giving him any sexy surprises tonight?" Thankfully, Thomas waited until Ethan was out of earshot to finally reference that God-forsaken text.

"Maybe," I lied, trying to save face.

I crossed my arms again. He just stared at me with that stupid smirk.

"What?" I asked defensively.

"Nothing," he shook his head with amusement. "It's just that my imagination has been running a little wild with what kind of sexy prizes Maura McCormick could possibly be specializing in."

I rolled my eyes.

"It's a shame my sarcasm didn't translate over text." I tried to sound as unaffected as possible.

There was a pause.

"Using the 'L' word with Ethan now," he observed.

"Yep," I said in a clipped tone, not inviting any further inquiries on the subject.

He rubbed the back of his neck.

"Well, I'm supposed to come out here and try to get you to come to Sunday dinner again, but..." he sighed, "we both know you're just going to turn down the invitation, right?"

"Thomas, I'm sor–"

"No, no, don't be sorry," he stopped me. "If anything, I think it's good that my mom finally saw you with Ethan so she can finally accept reality."

I nodded, trying to determine how he felt about the reality he was referring to. Not that it would change how I felt about Ethan. He took a step towards the church.

"But," he grinned, "that doesn't mean you still don't owe me that sexy prize."

And he was back to being a smartass.

THOMAS

After kissing Ashland on Saturday, I couldn't seem to get her off my mind. Hence the lame excuse of donating a box of my old paints and brushes to the youth center during my lunch break that Monday. I had been meaning to drop the stuff off for a while. It could have waited until Wednesday, but we would be replacing several parts of the engine that day and I wouldn't have the chance to talk to her.

The front desk was empty but I was pleased to see Ashland walk out after I rang the bell. The cleavage revealed by her fitted V-neck shirt made me even happier to see her.

When she saw me, she tilted her head back and slumped her shoulders down. She accepted that she had to face the consequences of what she'd revealed Saturday night. There was nothing better than knowing exactly where I stood with an attractive woman, especially when it required very little work.

"I thought I wasn't going to have to deal with this mortification until Wednesday." She smiled at me with chagrin.

"I assure you, I have no idea what you're talking about," I lied unconvincingly.

She raised an eyebrow at me. "Then how can I help you?"

"Is Maura here?"

"No, she and Sydney are at court today until about one." She gazed steadily at me.

"Oh, well, Maura had said that you guys ran an art program here, so I have some stuff to donate. Mostly paints and brushes. I checked all the paints; they're still usable."

She leaned in and looked down into the box I'd placed on the counter, giving me an even better view of her cleavage. I managed to shift my stare before she caught me looking.

"Is all of this yours?"

I nodded.

"You don't strike me as the artist type."

"Maybe that's why I'm donating it."

"No, my mom's an artist, and these are definitely brands of someone who's serious about it."

"What can I say? They were out of Tempera at the store."

She didn't laugh but continued to look at me.

"Well, thank you very much for the donation. I can let Maura know you stopped by."

I stared back, contemplating what else I could say to keep the conversation going.

"So," she started, "about Saturday..." She paused and laughed nervously. She was not used to being in the position of showing all her cards.

"Yes, about Saturday..." I mimicked but stopped, waiting to see what she would say.

"I feel like I should apologize for..." she searched for her words.

"Claiming that baseball is for pussies?" I filled in the blank. Her eyes widened.

"Oh, God," she sighed, leaning in towards the desk. "I did say that, didn't I?"

"Among other things," I confirmed.

She took a deep breath. "Well, clearly, I need to make it up to you. Do you have time for me to buy you some coffee?"

"Sure."

We stepped outside and began heading down the street. While we walked, I wasn't sure how much teasing she would let me get away with so I kept quiet. At least I wasn't the one who'd embarrassed myself.

"Do you have the day off?" she asked.

"No, just on my lunch break."

"No coveralls?" she said, referring to the t-shirt and jeans I was wearing.

"Nah, I seem to get harassed when I wear them outside of work. I hear some people call me Man-chanic behind my back."

Ashland looked over at me. I grinned.

"So, how long have you been a mechanic?" She coolly changed the subject.

"Uh," I paused, considering how to answer the question, "my dad started officially training me when I was fifteen, so if you go by that, twelve years...give or take a few years when I was living in New York."

I knew I only mentioned New York because she seemed like the type that might be impressed by it.

"Oh, did you go to school there?"

"No, I went here for school. I went to New York after I graduated because..." I trailed off. Talking about it now, I felt so removed from my past reasoning as a twenty-two-year-old.

"Because it's New York," she said with understanding.

"You ever been?"

"No, but I'd like to someday."

I held the door for her when we got to the coffee shop. She ordered and brought me my cup, and I followed her lead when she sat down at a table. After a few moments, I decided to make my move.

"So, Ashland the intern, what do you do when you're not kissing volunteers you run into at bars?"

"Not really much. Grad school has taken up all of my time lately."

"And I thought you were going to regale me with tales of winning beer pong tournaments and expert strategy for dominating at quarters," I joked.

"No," she laughed. "It's mostly been reading and writing papers when I'm not at the youth center or in class."

I looked at her with doubt.

"Saturday was actually the first time I'd gone out with my friends in over two months," she said and took a sip. She looked away, finally releasing me from her intense eye contact. Normally the amount of eye contact she made would make me nervous, but she was so attractive I found it appealing.

"It's a shame you're so busy. I was going to take you out," I said confidently. I sensed that was pretty much the only way to ask a woman like her out, at least when she wasn't drunk.

"Hmm," she smiled coyly. "Well, I'll have to think about it."

I nodded, unaffected by her pseudo-playing-hard-to-get.

"We should head back," she announced, glancing at the time. I grabbed my coffee and followed her out.

"So, if you were to take me out, where would we go? What would we do?" she asked while we crossed the street and made our way back to the center.

"Hmm," I pondered aloud. "Probably Thai food. You look like the Thai food type. And I would spend the majority of the time explaining the rules of baseball in a drawn out, condescending manner. I'd say we could go to a bar, but you seem to get a little handsy when you drink."

"And that's a problem for you?" she raised her brow, amused.

"Well, yeah," I said in an obvious tone. "It can be incredibly distracting when you're trying to explain what a ground-rule double is."

"So, Thomas the Man-chanic, I'm thinking if we're going to go out, I'm going to have to decide what we're doing, because you've already shown inferior judgment when it comes to sports."

I followed her up the steps to the front door. I had seen Maura's car in the parking lot and decided I would say hello to her before heading back to work.

"You're not the Thai food type?" I clarified, reaching above Ashland to hold the door for her as she opened it. She turned around. Her face was close and I thought she was going to kiss me again. She examined my face, considering what she wanted.

"Sushi," she announced definitively. She held my gaze, evaluating my response. I hated sushi, but there were some things I was willing to stomach when it came to good-looking women...and trying to sleep with them.

"Okay," I agreed.

"Wednesday?"

"Sounds good."

"Okay then. I'm glad we figured that out."

She turned and sauntered into the building. I was about to follow her when I heard someone calling my name. Justin was standing at the bottom of the steps. He looked timid after getting my attention.

"Hey, man, what's up?" I greeted, walking down the steps towards him.

It seemed like the best thing to do was pretend like the last time I saw him he hadn't looked like he was going to kill somebody. Justin looked down at his feet and took a breath before looking back up at me.

"I just wanted to apologize for last week."

He looked like he wanted to say more so I stayed where I was. He sighed again and looked slightly past me.

"I...um, was kind of going through some stuff...my mom got involved in drugs again and she threw me out...and there was some stuff that went on with Eric that had to do with the drugs my mom's boyfriend was dealing."

I nodded. The weight of his words registered as I realized he was only seventeen.

I didn't know how to respond and every possibility sounded awkward in my head. Should I tell him I understood when I had no life experience that would allow me to really understand? I stuck to nodding.

"I know that's no excuse for acting how I did...and I wanted to let you know that I hope I can come back to class."

"Sure...sure," I agreed, but realized this might be outside of my jurisdiction. "Did you talk it over with Maura or Sydney?"

"Yeah, we talked about it today on the way to court. Maura said she would meet with me and write up a contract before Wednesday, and if you were okay with it, I could come back."

He looked at me hopefully.

"Well, um, thank you for letting me know. I'm sorry that you're having to go through all that stuff, man."

Justin nodded.

"I was about to check in with Maura. I'll be sure to tell her we talked. So, I'll see you Wednesday then?" I reached out and shook his hand. That seemed like the best way to conclude the conversation.

"Thanks, man." He sounded relieved.

He gripped the straps of his backpack and walked away. I suddenly felt overwhelmed with thoughts about Justin and his life that had never crossed my mind before. How many times had he been separated from his mom because of drugs or something else? Did he have any other family? Would he ever graduate? The list of questions continued as I walked into the center to find Maura, convinced she was the only person who would make me feel better about all these new questions.

I found her standing by her desk scrolling through her phone. She was looking very professional in dress pants and a blue short sleeved blouse with her hair up in a bun. I looked like a teenager compared to her. I almost felt like one too, seeking out her guidance. I knocked quietly on the open door.

"Hey." She put her phone down. "Ashland said you wanted to donate all this stuff," she gestured to the box of paints and brushes on her desk. "Are you sure you want to do that?"

"Yeah, I'm sure. It was just sitting in a closet at my mom's house."

"But what if you decide you want to paint again? I mean, this all probably cost a lot."

It registered just how much money I had wasted anytime I had heard of a different paint or brush that was supposedly better for a different technique – meanwhile, there were people like Justin getting thrown out of their houses by their own mothers.

"Maura, it's fine. There's no reason for me to have all that any-more. There never really was. I kept a few things."

"Okay, well, we appreciate it." She looked at me. "You okay?"

"Uh, yeah," I looked away, feeling stupid that the nature of Justin's reality – and the reality of pretty much all the kids she worked with – was just now hitting me. "I ran into Justin outside."

"Oh."

"Yeah, he apologized for last Wednesday and said he wanted to come back." I finally made eye contact with her and she knew he had filled me in on the reason for his behavior. She reached out and touched my arm gently, moving past me to close the door.

"What did he share with you?" she asked, I assumed to keep from telling me more than I was supposed to know. The possibility of there being even more shitty information made me feel even more overwhelmed.

"Just that his mom was on drugs – again. And threw him out and that she was dating a drug dealer that Eric supposedly did something to. But that it was no excuse for how he acted and he was hoping I would let him come back to the garage."

"Kind of sucks when you find out some of the stuff that hap-pens to these kids outside of here." She looked at me understand-ingly, letting me know that my reaction was normal, even though stories like his were probably commonplace to her.

"I think of all the petty shit I was worried about or pissed off about when I was seventeen. My biggest concern was that I didn't want to work at my dad's shop on the weekends. Because why? I wanted to go paint fucking sunsets on the Sound. And some other kid's getting kicked out of his home by his own mother because she prefers getting high to having her own son around." The contrast left me depressed. "God, I am such an asshole," I declared, shaking my head.

Maura shrugged. "And when I was seventeen, I was devastated that my parents wouldn't send me on a class trip to Rome. Teenagers are incredibly self-centered and dramatic, even the at-risk ones," she said matter-of-factly. "Our perspective is based on our environment and what we're exposed to. I wouldn't be too hard on teenage Thomas. He didn't know he was an asshole," she kidded, trying to lighten the mood.

"That doesn't change the shitty situation that kid is in, through no fault of his own," I countered, surprised at how frustrated I sounded.

"You're right, it doesn't. But sitting around and reflecting about how shitty his life is doesn't really help either. I mean, it's good to appreciate that things don't come as easily for these kids, but you have to trust in their resiliency. Otherwise it just reinforces the message that things are hopeless and there's no reason to try."

I looked at her, seeking something more comforting. She read my expression.

"That's why it's great that we have a vocational program that's training Justin and others to have an employable skill, so hopefully they'll be in a better situation someday. Even if we could only find an asshole like you to teach it."

She looked at me, waiting for me to be amused. I wasn't offended, but I couldn't seem to smile.

"I'm sorry it's not like working on a car. There's no clear answer how to fix it."

"Well," I sighed, "speaking of fixing cars, I should probably get back to work."

I paused, wondering if she was going to hug me. After all the time I had spent relentlessly teasing her about her sensitivity, I longed for it in that moment. I was too proud to admit it though. I already felt like an idiot for not recognizing the severity of the lives of the kids I had been working with; no need to pathetically ask for a hug on top of it.

"Oh!" Maura exclaimed, her eyes lighting up. A grin spread across her face.

"What?" A smile finally appeared on my face when I looked at her.

"I have your prize!" she explained, opening a drawer.

Maura pulled out a thin eight by ten canvas and handed it to me. It was a paint-by-number picture of three unicorns by a water-fall. I was speechless.

"I wanted to give you one of my old latch-n-hooks, but apparently our garage flooded two years ago and all the yarn got moldy, so they had to be thrown out. You're lucky my mom stored all of my best work in my old room."

"Yes, lucky," I agreed sarcastically. "So, this is what you consider a sexy prize?" I laughed. After how embarrassed she'd been about the text, I was surprised she had even followed through on giving me something.

"Um, yeah. I mean, what's sexier than unicorns?" she said as if it were obvious.

I laughed and then impulsively pulled her in for a hug under the guise of thanking her.

"Thank you," I said, making sure not to hold on for too long. She backed away. She knew I was thanking her more for her counsel than anything.

"You're welcome," she said quietly, and then crossed her arms. "So, I will see you Wednesday then."

I nodded and opened the door.

"Have a good day." I looked at her one last time before leaving. My instinct had been right. She had made me feel better.

* * *

I had been so focused on working in the garage with the group on Wednesday that I hadn't thought that much about going out with Ashland afterwards. The fact that we were having sushi could have contributed to it, but it was also that the work we were doing on the engine was fairly advanced. After Monday, I had a newfound perspective on the value of the training I was providing. I was glad that Justin was back, but I had to accept that I would probably never see Eric again and wouldn't ever know why.

Ashland quietly walked into the garage when we were wrapping up for the evening. She joined Sydney on the counter, making sure to lock eyes with me. I was careful not to stare back for too long.

"Is this thing ever going to run again?" Juan asked, exasperated.

"We'll replace the radiator hose next week and then try it out," I shared my plan.

"Then we can drive it?"

"You got a permit, Juan?" Sydney asked, shutting down Juan's excitement. Judging by his expression, he didn't. "I suggest you work on that with your case manager before you break any laws."

"You're my case manager," he threw back at her.

"Well then I guess we have something to talk about next time we meet." She hopped down from the counter. "Make sure you guys put everything back."

I closed the hood of the car and answered a few lingering questions before dismissing everyone. The kids dispersed and Sydney stepped outside the garage, taking a moment to talk with River. Ashland continued to sit on the counter while I took inventory of the tools.

"Will you be wearing that out tonight?" she asked about my coveralls, still eyeing me. I walked over to the counter, locking up the tool cabinet next to it, and rested my hand on the counter next to her.

"You seem overly interested in my coveralls."

"What can I say? The blue-collar thing does it for me." She touched the name patch on my chest.

A smile slowly stretched across her face as she looked back into my eyes. Once again, I thought she was going to kiss me. There were still teenagers hanging out within eye shot of us, so I backed away.

"Well, unfortunately for you I brought a change of clothes." I started to walk out of the garage. She hopped down and followed me out. "I would look pretty ridiculous eating sushi while wearing this." I pulled the garage door down and locked it.

"Well, if I wasn't so hungry, I'd suggest we skip the sushi and go straight to the end of the night."

I let out a laugh, unable to think of a clever response. "I'm going to go change. I'll meet you by my truck?"

She nodded and headed toward the parking lot.

I went into the center and cleaned myself up. After changing into my jeans and a short sleeve polo, I stepped out of the bathroom and ran into Sydney in the hallway.

"Going out with Ashland tonight?"

"Yeah, we're going to go get a bite to eat."

She looked like she had something else she wanted to say so I waited.

"Look, Thomas, it's not really my philosophy to get into people's business..." she paused, "but, I have to remind you of the official program policy that certain types of relationships between staff and volunteers aren't allowed. But you guys are just getting food together, right?" She hinted at my need to agree with her.

"Yeah, yeah, of course."

Technically, it wasn't really a lie at that point, but after Ashland's comment by the garage, I would most likely sleep with her.

"Ashland's about four weeks away from finishing her internship here. I really don't want to have to dismiss all the work she's done this year should you guys start hanging out. So just make sure if and when you guys hang out, you do it off site."

I put together that when Sydney said 'hanging out' she meant 'sex or other physical contact.'

"She strikes me as the type who might get the idea that it would be exciting to hang out here, and I don't want to deal with that shit. Mostly because of the paperwork involved."

"Just so we're clear, you have a 'don't ask, don't tell' policy when it comes to me hanging out with Ashland?"

"I know, the irony is not lost on me," she admitted with a sigh. "All right then, good talk." She patted me on the arm and walked back to her office.

They would probably have me stop volunteering if a sexual relationship with Ashland became public knowledge. From the little I knew about Ashland, she would be anything but discrete if we slept together. Keeping it a secret seemed improbable. The kids' training would come to an end. All of their hard work wouldn't matter because of my inability to keep it in my pants. It was too big of a risk for what was at stake. So that settled it. I wasn't getting laid tonight.

It seemed best to wait and see what happened after dinner before breaking the news to Ashland. Despite her consistent flirting, I figured it would be presumptuous to announce that I was going to hold out on her before she had officially offered to go there. I mean, who starts off a date that way? Probably Maura. Okay, so what normal person starts off a date that way?

Going out with a woman when I wasn't completely consumed with the question of whether I was going to close the deal really took the pressure off. Putting all my effort into trying to impress a woman to the point of taking her clothes off could get exhausting. Luckily Ashland was an interesting person, so focusing on getting to know her better didn't seem like a chore.

She grew up in a commune in Portland with two hippy parents; her mother was an artist and her father was a writer. She was named after the town of Ashland in Oregon, where she was conceived during the Shakespeare Festival. It amused me that she knew this about herself and shared it in such a casual manner. I, on the other hand, had absolutely no desire to ever know where and when I, or either of my siblings, were conceived.

Her undergraduate degree was in Psychology from Evergreen College. Her alma mater wasn't surprising after hearing about her bohemian upbringing. She wasn't sure what she wanted to do after graduating with her Masters in Social Work, but wasn't stressed about it because she had another year of school to figure it out. I kept asking question after question about her, until she pointed out that we had been done eating for over an hour and were still at the restaurant.

She said she needed to get home because she had an early class the next day. Maybe her previous allusions to fooling around were all bravado. I wouldn't have to make any sort of announcement about how I couldn't sleep with her because it was against the rules. Good, I had worried about how lame I was going to sound anyway. We pulled up to her apartment building and I started to say goodnight.

"Well, you know," Ashland said while unbuckling her seatbelt, "the night doesn't have to end." She slid over next to me.

"I thought you had an early class?" My lips were inches from hers.

"I just wanted to get you out of the restaurant and back to my place," she admitted before pressing her lips against mine.

I kissed her back. She unbuckled my seatbelt and then started to kiss my neck, moving up to my ear.

"You have no idea how many times I've thought about this," she whispered. "And usually I picture us in this truck."

It was quite a revelation to know that Ashland had gone beyond checking me out to actually fantasizing about me. I pulled her head back so I could reclaim her mouth, my big speech about having to delay sex with her no longer at the forefront of my mind.

"I'd rather finish this upstairs tonight. We can save the truck for another time," she said in between kisses.

Her interjection made me pause long enough to remember what I was supposed to be doing – or rather, *not* doing. I backed away. Damn it. Why did I have to start being responsible now?

"What?" She stared at me, looking confused.

"We can't do this," I announced.

"What? Why? Shit, do you have a girlfriend?" she jumped to the most obvious conclusion.

"No," I shook my head and turned back to the steering wheel, trying to avoid looking at her in order to stick to my plan. "It's the youth center. They have a policy that staff and volunteers can't have inappropriate relationships."

"What's inappropriate about two consenting adults having sex?" she asked, mirroring my usual sentiment.

"If anyone found out, you could lose credit for your internship. I could be fired from volunteering. It would end the voc-ed program, at least for a while," I went over the consequences.

"But who says anyone has to find out?" She started to move back in.

"I really care about the voc-ed program," I managed to get out before she started kissing me again. "I don't want to do anything that would screw it up for those kids."

Ashland sighed heavily and rested back against the seat, crossing her arms.

"Leave it to a Catholic organization to put stupid stipulations on people's sex lives."

We sat in silence for a moment. I reached out and grabbed her hand.

"It's just until your internship ends."

"Ugh, that's like four weeks." Her annoyance was clear.

"I understand if you don't want to wait it out, but I don't mind just hanging out for the next month." I was being honest.

"You realize this shit about putting the kids first and wanting to date without getting laid for the next month only makes you more attractive?"

"What can I say? I'm a catch."

Ashland let out a whimper of frustration and sat up straight.

"Well, I guess I have no choice but to wait. It's those damn coveralls." She turned back to me after she got out of the truck. "I'll see you next week."

"Good night, Ashland." I didn't walk her to her door. My virtue would only go so far.

MAURA

My stupid phone woke me up. I reached out to my night stand, fumbling around to grab it, but still refused to lift my head. Ugh, I'd never realized how annoying my ringtone was. Finally, I got a hold of the damn phone. It was 6:34 a.m. and it was my dad.

"Hello?" I murmured. Suddenly my ear was filled with the blaring sound of my parents singing Happy Birthday. I pulled the phone away from my ear as I tolerated the gesture.

"Happy Birthday, Maurie!" my dad exclaimed. "Your mom and I are on our way to work and wanted to be the first to wish you a happy birthday—"

"Just like we've done since you were born!" my mom interrupted.

It was true. Ever since I'd moved out of the house, my parents made a point to call me as early as possible on my birthday so that they could maintain their title as the first people to wish me a happy birthday. Every year. Lucky for them, at twenty-six, my current streak of spinsterhood with no one to wake up next to had helped them keep the coveted title.

"Mmmhmm." I kept my eyes closed. "Thank you," I managed to get out.

"Do you feel older?" my dad predictably asked.

"Do you have any plans today?" my mom asked before I had a chance to answer my dad's question.

"I don't know," I mumbled, answering both of their questions.

"Well, we're very excited to take you out to dinner tonight with Ethan," my mom said loudly. Whenever using Bluetooth, my mom thought one was required to shout. "Do you think he got you anything special and sparkly for your birthday?"

The question produced an audible sigh from me.

"Well, I did ask for a tiara, so we'll see." I managed to be clever despite the early hour.

"He better not have gotten her a ring," my dad interjected. "He never asked my permission."

"Oh nonsense, James, people don't do that anymore," my mother said knowingly.

Considering what I knew about Ethan, she was dead wrong.

"I think a proposal is the perfect birthday gift, don't you, Maurie?"

"Mom, calm down. It's not happening today. Yes, Dad, he would ask your permission before asking me." I set them both straight, growing more tired the longer I stayed on the phone with them.

"Darn right he would," my dad agreed firmly.

"Is there anything else? Or can I go back to sleep?" I asked, knowing they wouldn't hold it against me.

"We will see you tonight at – what's the place called again?" I sensed my dad turning to my mom for help. "The Crow?"

"Just Crow, Dad," I corrected.

"Just Crow? It's called Just Crow?"

"No. Crow." I was now talking as loudly as my mom. "The restaurant is called Crow."

"Like we're eating crow?" my mom asked, trying to be funny.

I sighed dramatically.

"We'll see you at seven o'clock. Love you, Sweetie, and..."

"Happy Birthday!" they exclaimed in unison.

"Bye." I hung up and dropped the phone down on my bed. I didn't have to get up for twenty more minutes. Hopefully I could fall back asleep. It was highly unlikely, but that wasn't going to stop me from trying. Miraculously I managed to drift off for an extra ten minutes. It was better than nothing. Happy birthday to me.

Despite my parents calling so early and obnoxiously, there were worse ways to start my birthday. I straightened my hair and wore my favorite pair of jeans with a new shirt I'd recently bought. As I looked myself over in the mirror, I was pleased with the results of my extra effort for the day.

There was an arrangement of pink roses waiting for me on my desk at work. I read the accompanying card; they were from Ethan.

'Maura, Happy Birthday. Love, Ethan.'

I had never gotten an arrangement of flowers delivered to me, so it was exciting, even if the message wasn't. But...why did he pick roses? My favorite flowers were peonies.

Way to be ungrateful, Maura.

It was silly to get hung up on a grand gesture not being grand enough.

Stop being nitpicky and text him thank you. You have a great boyfriend who sent you roses.

"Hey, happy birthday, lady," Sydney gave me a rare hug upon entering our office.

"Thank you," I said.

"Who're the flowers from? Ethan?"

I nodded.

"Wow, fancy."

"I know. I don't think I've ever gotten flowers before."

"If only he knew he wasn't getting laid," she joked before moving over to her side of the office.

"Hilarious." I situated myself at my desk to begin work for the day. Although, I'd purposely planned a day with very little to do.

"Hope you don't have too much work today; we are heading to Teddy's promptly at four thirty." Sydney reminded me of our now four-year tradition of getting a beer at Teddy's before I had dinner with my parents.

The whole thing had started when I turned twenty-two. I was sitting in one of our graduate classes and starting to freak out because I was going to have tell my parents that I had once again broken up with a boyfriend that they were overly hopeful I would marry. Sydney decided the best way to solve it was to take me to Teddy's, get a few in me, and have me repeat the mantra 'Who the hell cares?'

"Oooh, we get to leave thirty minutes early?" I exaggerated my excitement.

"What can I say? I think I'm Ann's favorite," she playfully referenced my insecurity that our boss liked her best. "Actually, it has more to do with all the overtime we've been putting in prepping for the gala."

Every year the Archbishop hosted a gala where donors to various causes were honored and Catholic-affiliated nonprofits from the area also attended. The idea was to thank the benefactors, but also introduce them to those who worked at the funded nonprofits. It allowed the donors an opportunity to ask questions and get to know the programs better, but also increased the likelihood of getting additional financial support.

"I invited Ashland and Thomas out too. Hope that's cool," Sydney gave me a heads up.

"Of course, you know I'm all for as many people as possible celebrating my birth."

It would have been nice to see Thomas that day. I hadn't seen him in a couple of weeks. But it was a Thursday, not a Wednesday. Thomas would've had to switch shifts with someone to make it to Teddy's by four thirty and I really didn't think he would go out of his way like that just to have a drink with me on my birthday.

Too bad. Wait. Why do I care?

Okay, I seriously needed to get some work done.

On top of sending roses, Ethan called me during his lunch even though he was going to see me at dinner that night. He certainly shined as a boyfriend when it came to special occasions. He told me that he would be taking me out to dinner and the Seattle Symphony that weekend, because he wanted a chance to celebrate with only me.

I was caught off guard by his choice of activities since I had never expressed any interest in the symphony or classical music in general. Not that I was opposed to going. To avoid hurting his feelings or sounding unappreciative, I told him I was thrilled. Most women would find the gesture romantic.

"You ready to go?" Sydney said as soon as the clock hit four thirty.

"I thought you'd never ask." I practically jumped out of my seat.

Sydney beat me to Teddy's and was already at a booth with two beers when I arrived. Besides two other people sitting at the bar, the place was dead.

"What'd you order?" I asked, sliding into the booth.

"Stella."

I nodded. She knew me so well.

She held up her glass to clink with mine. "Happy birthday."

"Thanks." I took a drink.

"So...you and Ethan...how're things?" The specific tone she used turned it into a loaded question. It was one of the nuances that came with being close friends.

"They're good," I said, sounding chipper. Too chipper.

The questions were inevitable.

"You don't really talk about him much anymore," she observed.

"Well, is there anything in particular you would like to know?"

"Yeah, why haven't I met him?" she asked before taking a drink.

"Uh, there just hasn't been an opportunity, I guess," I lied.

The truth was I didn't know how Ethan was going to react to my closest friend being gay and I just didn't want to deal with it. Like all other areas of potential disagreement, I had been avoiding the topic. I was being a coward, but I couldn't bring myself to confess it to Sydney. She sensed it, but she took pity on me and didn't call me on it on my birthday. Eventually she would, and it would be justified.

An idea popped in my head.

"You know, you'll probably get to meet him at the gala next month," I said, practically gushing.

It would be the perfect opportunity for them to meet. Both Sydney and Ethan could agree that it was important to help those in poverty, and the event focused on that. The Archbishop would be there and the exhilaration from that alone would distract Ethan from caring about who Sydney was attracted to.

Brilliant, Maura, I congratulated myself.

And perhaps I needed to put more faith in Ethan. Wasn't it kind of small-minded of me to assume he wouldn't be accepting of people with views different than his own? He had never shown himself to be anything but a loving person.

"Looking forward to it. You know it's important that I make sure he's not a jerk."

"Well, Sean doesn't seem to care for him, so maybe that means you'll like him," I reasoned.

"Interesting. And what fault has the ever most Holy Father Finley found with him?"

"I don't know. He hasn't said it specifically, but last time I saw him he had all these questions about whether I was really happy...I don't know," I said again. "It was weird."

I held back from going into too much detail about what Sean had said because undoubtedly it would lead to Sydney posing the same questions. I had finally found a Catholic guy who was probably willing to marry me – couldn't people just let me have that?

"Sean just doesn't like to share his toys, even after he's done playing with them," Sydney evaluated.

"Gee, how insightful and objectifying of you to put it that way."

She shrugged, wearing a proud smile.

"Hey guys," Sydney greeted towards the door.

I turned to see Thomas and Ashland walk in.

"Not even five o'clock and already getting the party started. I like how you roll, McCormick," Thomas quipped.

"It's four fifty; we can round up." I was slightly disappointed when he sat down next to Sydney, leaving Ashland to sit next to me. "You didn't have to work?"

"I joined a baseball team that plays in Ravenna on Thursdays, so Michael switched the early shift with me, just for the season."

"Baseball team?" I said curiously, never having pictured Thomas as the type who would willingly participate in a community activity.

"Yep, they needed an outfielder, I got Finley-ed into it," he joked. "So, what're we drinking?"

"Stella," Sydney answered.

"You know what you want?" he asked Ashland while he got up.

"Stella sounds good to me," she said sweetly.

The way she was looking at him was a little too friendly for my liking. Then he smiled back. I glanced over at Sydney who was already staring at me. Ashland's eyes noticeably followed Thomas while he made his way to the bar.

"So, how was your day, Ashland?" Sydney called her attention back to our table.

"Oh, fine...just, you know, class, nothing special. I'm ready for summer."

"That's right, you're only with us for two more weeks," Sydney acknowledged. "I'll have to make sure and remind all the teens."

"Oh, trust me, I started the countdown with them like five weeks ago."

Thomas returned with the pints and sat back down next to Sydney.

"I was going to ask if I'm supposed to attend that gala thing? It's on the last week of my internship, but it's the night of my last day, so I didn't know what was expected."

"Well, since you worked on putting everything together, we would really like it if you could go, but no, you're not required," Sydney said. "There'll be a lot of other nonprofits there, so it might be a good opportunity to network for next year," she added.

"Hmm," Ashland considered Sydney's words. "I'll think about it."

She acted like she would be doing us a favor if she showed up. I wanted to uninvite her to the damn thing. Sydney sensed my frustration and changed the subject.

"So, Thomas, you play ball?"

"Yes, ma'am. But not really after high school. What about you?"

"Yeah, I played softball in high school, second base."

They briefly exchanged a couple of names to see if they knew different players from our alma maters. It would have been polite to ask Ashland if she played softball or any sport in high school, but I didn't care.

"Cool. What about you, Maura? Were you on the softball team?"

Sydney snickered at Thomas' question. He looked back over at her, then at me.

"No, I did not," I said calmly. "Apparently, Syd finds it amusing that someone could even consider it a possibility."

"You should watch her try to hit a ball. It's pretty hilarious," Sydney informed. "Luckily, by the fifth grade her dad got her to stop twirling like a ballerina when she swung the bat. It still didn't help much with being able to make contact with the ball."

Thomas tried unsuccessfully to suppress a grin.

"Excuse me, it is my birthday. You have to be nice to me."

"But it's so much more fun to pick on you, Maura," he said matter-of-factly.

"Exactly," Sydney agreed.

"Whatever," I dismissed them, knowing their teasing was a sign of affection.

"So, where's my buddy, Ethan?" Thomas asked, looking around. He didn't sound sarcastic, but I knew he was being sarcastic.

"He's still at work," I said.

"Wait, so Thomas has met Ethan and I haven't?" Sydney clarified. I opened my mouth, but Thomas started talking before I could explain.

"Oh, several times," he exaggerated.

"Hmm, interesting," Sydney reflected. "And what would you say is your evaluation of him, Thomas? Since Maura's been so secretive with him, I'll have to rely on your opinion."

A grin spread across Thomas' face as he considered his words. I let out a sigh, anticipating a snarky reply.

"Hmm, what would I say about Ethan?" he paused, gazing steadily at me.

Great, here comes another virgin joke.

"You know, Sydney, there's not much I can say about him, other than that he seems like a safe choice for our Maura here. Especially in this day and age with all the technology. Always a good idea to have a friend who can fix your computer for free. I mean, it's not as useful or manly as, say, someone who can fix your car, but you know, to each their own."

He finished off his drink.

"What time is it?" He pulled out his phone and looked at it. "I actually have to get going to my game. Are you finished?" He pointed at Ashland who still had half of her beer left. She nodded and stood up.

"I promised Ashland I'd let her observe the social dynamics of washed-up athletic males," he joked while he got up from the table. He and Ashland may not have been holding hands, but they were standing awfully close.

"All right, well, happy birthday, Maura. Don't get too wild tonight." His sarcasm was obvious that time.

After they left, I waited a moment, staring at my drink before I started in with Sydney.

"Okay, seriously, what the hell was that?" I asked. I wanted her to validate my outrage, but I knew her better than that. Sydney rarely responded to things with heightened emotion, especially things as petty as relationship drama.

"What?" she acted clueless. I could tell she was holding something back.

"Those two," I exclaimed in a hushed tone, not wanting the other people there to look over at me. "They're clearly hooking up," I declared.

"I don't see how that's any of our business."

I examined her face.

"You know they're hooking up, don't you?" I stared her down. "Don't you?"

She sighed, knowing I would just keep asking if my suspicion wasn't validated soon.

"I don't know anything. I just know that they went out to dinner last Wednesday after work. But I told Thomas the policy regarding staff and volunteers and said if they were going to do anything, it would be best to do it on the down low. We came to a 'don't ask, don't tell' agreement."

"Really? 'Don't ask, don't tell?' You?"

"I'm more in favor of that than a witch hunt. And it's not like they were bad while they were here. I didn't see any grab-ass, did you?"

"No, but that's not the point," I said without having my point ready.

"And what is the point, Maura?"

Damn it. Sydney knew I didn't have one. My knee was fidgeting while I considered the two of them together.

"Is there any reason why it would be so upsetting should Thomas and Ashland decide to get together? Any reason at all?" Sydney prompted.

I sensed what she was hinting at while she leveled her stare at me. I took a deep breath and got my leg to stop bouncing.

"No," I said calmly. "I just don't like it when people break the rules."

"Yes, clearly that's what has gotten you so upset about the situation."

We let a silence pass. She took a drink.

"So...doing anything special with your hair tonight?"

The question sounded so absurd coming from her, I let out a laugh.

"What? Jules told me to work more on my people skills."

I shook my head.

"I'll be sure to let her know that you're trying."

With that, Sydney had moved us past the moment of tension and returned us to enjoying the rest of our tradition. She knew I wasn't ready to admit that Thomas popped up in my mind more than I wanted him to. Normally I would confide everything to her: uncertainty about Ethan, confusion about Thomas...but over the past several weeks, I had decided to close myself off from her when it came to the whole matter. Somewhere along the line I had decided that if I voiced any of the thoughts floating in my head, it would make them real. I desperately didn't want that.

What I wanted was to be settled. God knows it had taken long enough to get to this point. I did not need to mess it up with my own stupid second-guessing. And processing with Sydney would only give credence to what was in my head. Taking Ethan to dinner with my parents was the best remedy for the entire situation. If anyone could convince me of Ethan's attributes and the logic of loving him, it would be my grandbaby-hungry parents.

I returned home to get ready for dinner before Ethan picked me up. I was finishing my makeup when there was a knock at the door. I looked through the peephole to see him standing there.

"Hi." When I opened the door to let him in, I noticed he was holding a narrow box almost as tall as he was, wrapped with a bow.

"Hey." He stepped into my apartment and kissed me hello. "I was able to sneak in. I guess I don't look too shady tonight," he joked.

I looked over his outfit; a full suit and tie. I wondered if Ethan had ever looked shady in his entire life.

"Happy birthday," he said for the fourth time that day. "You look beautiful," he commented on my black, tea-length, dress.

"Thank you." I adjusted the clasp on my necklace, a solitary diamond my parents had gotten me for my graduation four years ago. They probably didn't think at the time that it would still be the only diamond I owned.

Shut up, Maura. Look, he brought you a present.

"Yes, this is for you." He noticed my stare. "Sorry if I should've waited for dinner, but I thought it would be a little awkward to haul this through the restaurant."

He tilted the box over to me.

"Do you want me to open it now?"

"Yes, yes, of course," he eagerly granted permission.

I tore the paper, legitimately curious as to what it could possibly be.

Skis.

I immediately schooled my expression to mirror the excitement on his face.

"Wow, skis." I kept my exclamation factual.

"Yeah, I assumed you probably didn't have your own pair yet. And you really can't go wrong with Rossignol. I made sure they were purple." His expression revealed how proud he was of himself.

I kept the smile pasted on my face.

"Of course, you'll need a suit to go with it. But I figured, being a woman, you would probably want to pick that out yourself. That's the other part of your present. This Saturday before we go to the symphony, we can go to REI and you can pick out whatever you like."

He paused.

"You look a little confused."

I guess the convincingness of my smile had begun to fade.

"Well," I tried to think quickly. Saying I was confused that he got me equipment for an activity that I hated would crush him. I couldn't be that cruel.

"It's just that it's the end of May...and I wasn't expecting to do much skiing this summer," I said.

He let out a laugh. This was the closest to giddy that I had ever seen Ethan.

"Of course not," he agreed. "But I wanted to make sure you would be ready when you come with me and my family to Vail this Thanksgiving," he informed me...which I guess was supposed to count as an invitation.

My eyes widened at the unexpectedness of the whole situation.

This amused him. "And I bet you thought I wasn't good at surprises."

He pulled me in for a deep, long kiss while I continued to hold the skis. I was grateful that the kiss was nice enough that it distracted me from the anxiety I had started to feel from all the plans he had thrown at me within the span of three minutes.

I envisioned Ethan and me sitting by a fire at some extravagant ski lodge and him ultimately proposing. I tried to block out the accompanying visions of me repeatedly falling on my ass in the snow while trying to ski down a stupid hill with all the experienced skiers passing and cursing at me for being in the way. It was hard to tell if it was a vision or a memory from childhood. Ethan broke away and stared into my eyes, tucking my hair behind my ear.

"So," he sighed. "We'd better get to dinner."

I nodded, slowly backing away.

"Just let me grab my coat." I handed the skis over to him, unsure of the right way to store them for the time being.

Ethan was the most talkative I'd ever seen him while we drove to the restaurant. He held my hand the whole way there. He talked at length about his family's tradition of going to Vail every Thanksgiving since he was ten. I tried my best to get myself as excited as he was about the whole thing. I did a pretty good job faking it, since he just kept talking. In my gut, I didn't feel right about the situation. I didn't want to go. What bothered me most was that I couldn't figure out the exact reason why. It felt like there was more to it than the fact that I didn't like skiing and I didn't like the cold.

"You're awfully quiet. Are you okay?" He finally noticed my lack of involvement in the conversation.

"Well," I paused, "I was just thinking about Saturday, and I think it might be kind of a pain to go try on a bunch of ski suits when I'm all dressed up and my hair's done." This was by far the most high-maintenance thing that I had ever said. "So maybe we can do it another time? I'm sorry. I know that sounds incredibly vain."

"No worries," he said. "We can do it anytime you'd like."

"Plus, there will probably be more sales if we wait closer to the season," I rationalized. He looked over to me and smiled.

"Did I ever tell you how attractive frugality is in a woman?"

"Yeah, I know you like your women cheap," I quipped with a grin.

He raised an eyebrow at me, but didn't smile.

"Have you ever eaten at this place before?" he changed the subject. We turned down the street the restaurant was on.

"No. Sydney recommended it."

I remembered what I had told Sydney about Ethan going to the gala. "So, in two weeks, the Archbishop is hosting a gala for benefactors and local non-profits. Do you want to be my date?" I asked as he parked the car.

"It would be my pleasure." He kissed the back of my hand as he held it.

"Great." I smiled, trying to ignore the feeling in my stomach.

We walked into the restaurant hand in hand and saw my parents already sitting at the table. I don't think Ethan noticed my mom eyeing my left hand. Thank God. I was sure to give her a subtle look of warning. She didn't let the absence of a ring detract from the look of joy plastered on her face.

"Happy Birthday, Maurie," she exclaimed as she pulled me in for a big hug, more excited about my birthday than I was. When she let me go, I turned to my dad, who played it a little cooler than my mom.

"Happy Birthday, Sweetheart." He gave me a quick kiss on the cheek before turning to Ethan to shake his hand.

Fortunately, my parents had already ordered a bottle of wine and an appetizer. Perfect. I planned to eat and drink away the anxiety that had been unwrapped with those stupid skis. Sydney had not done me wrong by recommending this place; if there was ever a place to eat feelings, it was Crow. I mean, really, how could anyone feel anything but good when eating bacon wrapped, goat-cheese-stuffed dates? It was helpful that my mother managed to hold back from asking or saying anything embarrassing.

It was toward the end of dinner when Ethan mentioned his plans – well, I guess they were technically our plans, that I'd had no say in making, to go to Vail for Thanksgiving with his family. He turned to me and I instinctively mimicked his smile like I had been doing all night. My parents were not as quick to provide positive feedback.

"As in 'Colorado?'" my dad clarified.

"Yes. My family's been going there for years," Ethan said happily. "I think Maura will be a perfect addition to our Thanksgiving tradition."

There was a pause. It turned into an awkward silence. My mom slowly forced a smile. I think this was the first time it registered for her, and possibly my dad, that if I was ever going to have a spouse it would mean not spending every major holiday together.

Ethan turned to me, unsure of what to make of my parents' reaction. Before I could change the subject, our waiter came out with a piece of tiramisu with a candle in it. He placed it in front of me and very coolly wished me a happy birthday. It was too classy of a place to have the whole wait staff sing Happy Birthday. The one time in my life when that would've been helpful. I looked to my dad for help.

"Well, go ahead, Maurie, make a wish," he encouraged.

I blew out the candle but failed to make a wish.

"You know," my dad began, "tiramisu is Maura's favorite dessert next to ice cream," my dad began, turning to Ethan.

I knew immediately what story was going to follow.

"The first time she had it, we were at a family wedding and she was ten. Her cousin Greg, who was I think sixteen at the time, told her he was going to call the police on her because it had alcohol in it and it was against the law for minors to consume alcohol. She was certain they were coming to lock her up."

My dad's story managed to get my mom to smile genuinely again.

"She felt so guilty, she tracked the priest down at the reception and asked if he would hear her confession."

"It took us a few weeks to convince her she hadn't broken any laws," my mom added.

"Well," Ethan squeezed my hand, "you did an incredible job forming her conscience."

I didn't feel like this was an entirely true statement, but the taste of the tiramisu helped me cope with my internal objection.

We were able to make it through the rest of dinner without any more awkward pauses. I hoped my dad would talk my mom down enough after dinner to avoid getting a guilt-ridden phone call the next day. As Ethan drove me home, I wondered if he was going to want to hang out some more or if the night would end once we got to my apartment. I found myself hoping for the latter.

Wasn't that wrong? If this was a person I loved, shouldn't I want to spend as much time with him as I could, especially on a day like my birthday? But if he came back to my apartment, it would turn into me wanting to make out and him not allowing it, or as much of it as I wanted, and then me ultimately feeling ashamed for any advances I had made.

"So," he called me out of my head, "it didn't seem like your parents were too excited for you to come to Vail."

"It just caught them off guard, that's all."

"We've been dating for a while now. I hoped they'd be excited by it. I mean, usually it's a sign that a particular question is about to be asked, followed by a particular announcement," he hinted. This was the closest Ethan had ever come to mentioning plans to ask me to marry him. Something I thought I was longing for until about three hours ago.

"I'm their only child. If they don't see me on a major holiday, it's kind of a huge change for them." I left out that it was for me, too.

"Yet they went on a cruise on Easter," he countered. His tone was even, and a rational person wouldn't have taken it to be confrontational.

"Thanksgiving is a bigger deal than Easter in my family." I tried my best to mirror his unemotional tone.

"You do realize one is a secular holiday and one celebrates the resurrection of Christ?" he said matter-of-factly.

"No, I didn't. I guess it was all those years in public school that confused me."

Sarcasm. Always a mature way to respond, Maura.

But it seemed pointless to debate with him why my family was justified in making a bigger deal about Thanksgiving than Easter.

"I'm just surprised that they were caught off guard, given that I invited you to a more significant holiday already when I invited you to Easter."

"Well, I guess it's good they have six months to get used to it," I said, really talking more about myself than I was my parents. Maybe I would feel differently about the whole thing as time passed. He pulled up to my building and turned to me.

"So, what now, Birthday Girl?"

I was unwilling to invite him upstairs until he suggested it himself.

"You want me to take you somewhere else?"

"Honestly, I'm kind of tired."

It was only nine o'clock, but in my defense, it was a weeknight. He affectionately put his hand on my cheek.

"Fair enough. We'll save the rest of our celebrating for Saturday." He leaned in and kissed me politely. "Happy birthday."

"Thank you. Have a good night." There was a small wave of relief that he didn't offer to walk me to my door.

All the events of the night were replaying over and over in my head as I took the elevator to my floor. As soon as I entered my apartment, I kicked off my heels and changed out of my dress. Why the hell was my brain reacting like this when everything I'd always wanted was finally happening? This was not a normal reaction to have. Of course, now I wanted to talk to Sydney about it.

Way to be consistent.

It was too late to call her.

And I couldn't even formulate what I was upset about anyhow. *My boyfriend invited me to Thanksgiving with his family. How dare he?* I would sound like a crazy person. I was being crazy. Leave it to me to find the perfect situation and then find something wrong with it. This was all Sean's fault. I wasn't sure how it was, but I'd be up all night anyway, so I had time to figure out some way to blame him for how unsettled I was.

THOMAS

I walked in from the outfield after the third pitch ended in a strike for the opposing team's batter at the end of the seventh inning. I high-fived a few of my teammates whose names I barely knew before tossing my glove in my bag. Ashland was watching me from the sidelines. No stranger to bravado, I winked at her. My confidence was helped by the fact that I'd had four hits and a three-run homer in the sixth that led to our victory.

"Good game, man." Father Sean patted me on the back while I took a drink of water. I nodded and hoisted my gym bag over my shoulder. "Are you coming to the bar with us?"

I saw Ashland gathering her blanket and walking towards me.

"Nah, man," I declined. "I think I have to get this one home to study," I motioned to her as she approached.

"Ashland!" he greeted gregariously. "Great to see you again."

She shook his hand. I could tell she was embarrassed about the things she had said to him the last time she'd seen him. Father Sean was polite enough not bring any of it up. "You must be this guy's lucky charm. He couldn't hit worth a damn last game."

I was surprised by his word choice, but I couldn't argue with the truth of the statement. I was zero for five during that last game. Luckily, I'd been able to pick off a few fly balls to prove my worth my first time out.

"We'll see you next week." He gave me another hard pat on the back before heading off with the other players.

"So, what now?" I asked Ashland. We both knew what we really wanted to do. I tried to come up with an alternative. "Are you hungry?"

She shrugged. "I have food and beer back at my place. I don't really want to waste money."

"Fair enough."

Ashland humored me by allowing me to recap the game as I drove her home, although I'm certain it was the last thing she wanted to talk about. She led me upstairs to her studio apartment, further stroking my ego by asking about my glory days. I walked into her apartment, rambling on about the time I hit the ball out of the park at a game in Tumwater.

"Why don't you have a seat," she invited, "and I'll see what I have."

She briefly disappeared into the kitchen, returning with two opened beer bottles. A layer of clothing had also been taken off, revealing a fitted white tank-top.

"So, I don't really have a lot of food like I thought did," she admitted, handing me a beer and sitting down next to me on the couch. "But beer has plenty of calories, right?"

She took a drink. I mirrored her action, trying not think about the meal my mom had at home for me. It didn't help that the beer was a Rolling Rock. She caught my eyes looking her over.

"It gets so hot up here in the afternoon lately. There have been days where I don't even put pants on," she said nonchalantly. I let the comment drop, reminding myself that I was not having sex with her that night. This didn't prevent me from picturing her walking around her apartment half naked though.

"You want me to look in your fridge and see if I can throw something together?" I offered, confident in my skills to create a whole meal out of random ingredients.

"You know how to cook?"

"It's the only way to survive living in New York on a budget."

She put her bottle down on the coffee table, then took the bottle out of my hands and placed it next to hers. Ashland had no interest in feeding me. I stayed silent. It was rude to turn down an advance before it happened, right?

We began kissing. I leaned back on the couch and she maneuvered herself on top of me. Instinctively, I moved my hands around her hips while she trailed her lips down to my neck. I willed myself from going any further, my hands glued to her hips. In my opinion, my level of self-control was impressive. Definitely new territory for me.

"Are you sure you're not hot?" she started to pull up my shirt.

"No. I think I'm good." The words sounded unconvincing as they came out of my mouth.

"I can't believe you told me we have to wait a whole month," she whispered in my ear before pulling herself up slightly to see my face.

"Isn't it only two more weeks now?" The small strap of her tank top had fallen off her shoulder. I moved it back up, taking every precaution that she remained clothed.

"No one has ever made me wait," she said, kissing me again. It seemed like this factor turned her on.

"I guess you're just going to have to deal with it," I said unapologetically, enjoying the small amount of power I gained from the whole situation. It was a welcomed change from the days of being an easily aroused undergrad begging for whatever I could get.

Ashland kissed me harder, pressing her pelvis against one of my legs. I had to sit up at that point, which was mentally harder to do than physically, seeing as she didn't weigh much. She kneeled on the couch, draping her slender arms around me.

"If you want to head over to the bed, I could give you a massage."

I smiled at her offer, almost in disbelief that she was trying so hard.

"While that sounds amazing," I put my hand around hers and patted it, "I think I'd better go."

"Seriously, Thomas, what's the big deal?" she sighed as she broke away but continued to look at me. "No one has to know. I can keep a secret, can't you? What? Are you going to go tell on me to Father What-A-Waste when you go to confession?"

I laughed at her question.

"I don't go to confession. And Sean's not the one you need to worry about when it comes to losing credit for your internship. Is two weeks really going to kill you? I mean, if it is, we can go out to a bar right now. It really won't be that hard to find a guy who's willing to sleep with you, not with that ass. But I feel I should warn you that whoever you find won't be nearly as satisfying as me. And probably won't look as good in coveralls."

She groaned dramatically and put her head on my shoulder.

"I just don't understand why we can't just keep it between us," she made one last attempt to rationalize it to me.

"On the small chance that it should come up, I'm just not willing to lie."

In all reality, the truth was that I specifically wasn't willing to lie to Maura. At this point in our friendship, Maura could tell when I was holding something back. She would be disappointed in me if I put my volunteer status at risk to sleep with Ashland.

She tilted her head, continuing to stare at me intently. I fought the urge to kiss her.

"Go," she instructed, accepting her defeat. "Before I jump you again."

I grabbed my keys and walked towards the door. I turned to her before letting myself out. "You want to hang out this weekend?"

"Not unless you're having sex with me," she said bluntly.

"I'll text you," I laughed.

MAURA

I stood in my running clothes, staring down at the two dresses I had laid out earlier that morning. I'd thought that going for a run in the afternoon would provide clarity for the decision of what to wear, or at least the perspective of how much I was overthinking the whole thing. It hadn't.

Although I had never been to the symphony, I knew it warranted more formal attire. Unfortunately, I had already worn my one simple black dress on my birthday, and that left me with only two other choices: the floral lavender sundress I wore for Easter, or an old bridesmaid dress I had saved, despite never having worn it since the wedding.

The bridesmaid dress was one that I had always wanted to wear again. It was navy and had a chiffon overlay that was draped over the chest Grecian style with shirring at the waist. I always thought I looked good in the dress, but the draping of the chiffon fabric resulted in a deep V-neckline. In all fairness, there was a satin underlay with a sweetheart neckline so it wasn't like it showed off a lot...but something about the overlay exposing the underlay made me hesitate on the rare occasions I had the opportunity to re-wear it.

So, I should just go with lavender dress. But it was a sundress, and didn't that rule out wearing it at night? So, the navy dress was perfect. It was the most formal thing I owned that didn't look straight out of a prom catalog.

Why do brides always do that? I mused, considering my options. *They say they'll pick a bridesmaid dress that you can wear again, like they're doing you a favor, and then it ends up being some random color and floor length. Who wears a floor length gown to anything but a wedding or prom? Brides are delusional. Except Sara,* I nodded to myself to be fair. *She picked the navy bridesmaid dress. Good job, Sara. Okay, I want to wear the navy dress...but the neckline.*

My gut was telling me Ethan would think the navy dress was too revealing. I opened my closet to examine whether I had anything else that could potentially work. There was a black flared skirt that I usually paired with a white fitted blouse. I pulled the combination out and laid it next to the dresses. It looked so plain compared to the other two. I let out a sigh just as my phone buzzed.

> Are you home? I have something I
> wanted to drop off for you.

It was Thomas. I was thankful for the distraction. So grateful, I refrained from analyzing what could possibly lead him to needing to come to my apartment to give me something on a Saturday.

> Yes. I'm home until about six.

I glanced around my room and the living room to make sure there wasn't anything I had to clean up. Of course not. I had been so anxious since my birthday, the whole place was immaculate. I guess there were worse nervous habits to have than cleaning.

> Address?

I sent him my address, then took a break from staring at the dresses and sat on my couch. Normally I would have cared that I was having a guest over and hadn't showered, but it was just Thomas.

To avoid going back into my bedroom to stare at the outfits, I went through my phone. Did I have enough time to head to the mall and find another dress? Like I could commit to buying anything in such a short amount of time. Thomas texted me to say he was outside.

Well that was quick.

I buzzed him in.

When he made his way up, I saw he was holding a flat package, wrapped in brown paper. He was also dressed in athletic clothes.

"Did you go running without me?" he asked with feigned offense.

I stepped back and opened the door wider.

"Come on in." I ignored his question. I wished I could still go on runs with him without upsetting Ethan.

"So, this is where Maura lives," Thomas reflected as he walked in.

I waited for the inevitable joke.

"It's nice."

I stared at him, still expecting a dig.

"I mean, I would have expected more rosaries and statues of Mary, but it's still nice." There it was.

"Looks like you went running too," I commented on his clothes, picturing him jogging with Ashland, marveling at all her stupid Portland stories.

"Actually," he said matter-of-factly, "I'm on my way to meet Father Sean at the batting cages."

"Well aren't you two becoming the best of friends," I said flatly.

"Maybe he's taken me on as a pet project. They probably have some sort of adopt-a-heathen program running during Ordinary time," he cleverly referenced the Church calendar.

Thomas walked further into my apartment, eventually looking into my bedroom. "So, this is where the magic doesn't happen," he continued to joke. "What's with all the clothes? Are you planning on putting on a private fashion show for Ethan later?"

I shook my head. "We're going to the symphony tonight. I was trying to figure out what to wear."

He looked over the three outfits.

"You wanna model them for me?" he smirked, knowing my answer.

"No."

"So," he paused, looking back at the clothes. "Which one is Maura leaning towards? Nun In Training, the Easter Repeat, or this –" he picked up the navy dress and held it up in front of me, "surprisingly sexy little number."

I quickly grabbed the hanger from his hands and rolled my eyes. I immediately ruled it out as an option. If Thomas labeled the dress as sexy, then Ethan would surely think it was over the top.

"If you're trying to get to third base, then I would definitely go with that one," he winked, maintaining his stupid grin.

I sighed and tossed the dress back down on the bed.

"Besides giving me fashion advice, why did you need to come here?" I stared at him expectantly.

"Happy birthday." He handed over the package. "I wanted to give it to you on Thursday, but it wasn't finished being framed."

He watched me as I unwrapped it.

I couldn't think of anything else it could be besides a painting, but I didn't believe he would have painted something just for me. I turned the frame around to see the canvas and my mouth dropped open when I saw it. It was a statue of Saint Jude, but it was *my* Saint Jude, the one from Blessed Sacrament.

Like the Pike Place Market picture, Thomas had captured the lighting perfectly. There were sun rays coming down from the stained-glass windows in the background, hitting the statue and illuminating it along with the candles that surrounded. I had always thought the scene was beautiful, but I'd never thought it could be translated into a painting. Speechless, I looked up at him.

"It's the only location in that horribly dark and depressing church with decent lighting. I never noticed until I saw you sitting over there at Easter," he explained casually.

I remained silent, still having trouble formulating words.

"Anyway, when my mom told me that was the patron saint of lost causes, I thought it was a pretty appropriate thing for me to paint for you," he laughed.

"Thomas..." I started, but found myself stopping, transfixed by what I held in my hands. I tried to remember if I had ever told him that it was my favorite place to sit at church or that St. Jude was one of my favorite saints. I couldn't recall ever saying anything to him. As I continued to notice the details, it registered how much time he must have spent working on it...for me. My silence didn't seem to bother him.

"This is amazing," I finally said. "This must have taken you -"

"Really, it was nothing," he downplayed.

"But you said that you don't paint anymore."

He shrugged.

"My sister asked me to paint a mural of Cinderella's castle for Sophie's first birthday party, so I thought this was a good way to get back into the swing of things."

I gave him a look of doubt but decided not to challenge him.

"Well, thank you...it's beautiful." I looked directly into Thomas' eyes.

"I know it's not the Seattle skyline or Mount Rainier, but..." he shrugged again, "I guess I wanted to try something new. Don't tell my mom," he laughed. "She's been trying to get me to paint Jesus and his friends for years. So, what's with the skis?" He nodded to the corner where I had stashed them. "You planning a summer trip to the Alps? I hear those are better in the winter."

"Oh, uh, those are from Ethan. For my birthday," I said, trying to make my tone sound even.

Thomas inspected my face. "Even though you hate skiing?"

I nodded. He raised an eyebrow at me.

"His family goes to Vail every Thanksgiving, and I'll be joining them. It's very thoughtful," I attempted to sound convincing, either for myself or for Thomas; I'm not sure who.

It was obvious to me that Thomas' gift was better without him even trying. I could tell by the look in his eyes that he knew that too.

"And he's taking me to the symphony tonight," I added, placing the painting down and starting to exit my room, hinting at Thomas to follow me to the door. "Ethan seems to really go all out when it comes to birthdays."

"I didn't know you were a fan of the symphony," Thomas commented, walking behind me, the doubt evident in his voice.

"It should be fun," I said breezily. "At least more fun than going to the batting cages with Sean." I opened the door for him.

"I don't know, if I end the night watching Seven Brides for Seven Brothers with my mom, it could be a tie," he teased while he walked out the door. "Have fun tonight. Text me when you get bored," he said cockily. "Happy birthday."

"Thank you for the painting," I said with composure. "Have a good night."

He nodded and turned to walk down the hallway. I let out a large sigh once I was concealed behind my door.

I returned to my bedroom, allowing myself some time to stare at the painting. The painting of one of my favorite places that Thomas had made just for me.

Don't read into it. It had to be just a coincidence.

There was no way he could have known how special that statute was to me. Whether it was just a fluke or not, that didn't change the fact that I loved the painting more than anything I had been given in a long time.

I propped the frame up on my nightstand. I returned to the remaining clothes on the bed and quickly decided that I would wear the conservative skirt and blouse. If I wore the lavender dress, all I would think about was how the last time I'd worn it, Thomas had decided to paint again...for me.

THOMAS

It was so busy at the batting cages that Father Sean and I ended up sharing a cage. He graciously allowed me to go first. Wanting to guarantee several hits, I set the pitch speed to a less-than-challenging level. I'm not sure what catharsis I needed, but it was therapeutic hitting ball after ball.

"So," Father Sean called out after I had made it through about half of my pitches, "how're things going with Ashland?"

"Fine," I said as I swung and hit the ball harder.

"She seems nice."

"Yep."

With Father Sean, I didn't know what type of details I was expected to divulge. If it were Tyler or Jeremy, or pretty much any other man, they would be looking for the rundown of breasts, ass, and what she was like in bed. In this circumstance, I would get hassled for not having any information about any of those. Father Sean waited for a few more pitches before trying again.

"So, do you like her?"

I hadn't been asked that by another guy since high school. Dumbfounded by the unfamiliarity of the question, I let a pitch go by.

"Uh, yeah, I guess. She's fine." I tried to answer quickly and regain my focus for the next pitch. I swung and missed.

"You're not one to get smitten," he evaluated with a laugh.

I shrugged and looked at him, not caring at this point that I let another pitch go by. "I don't know. I don't not want to hang out with her."

"I'm guessing that's not how you've phrased it to her," he responded flatly.

I was finally able to make contact with a ball again, but it was a bad hit. "What do you want to know, man?" I called him out.

"Nothing," he said simply. "Just making small talk."

He shifted his feet, standing with his arms crossed. "I didn't expect you to still be hanging out with her after you hooked up the night of the M's game."

I shook my head, smiling. "Such low expectations of me, Father."

"Oh, bullshit," he retorted. "You were all about the hit it and quit it philosophy that night."

"I do believe you said I had to act like a gentleman before you left. Are you saying you think I acted in any other manner?" I took my last pitch, pleased that I ended with a nice hit.

"No," he corrected as he took my place in the cage, taking a few warm up swings. "I'm saying I'm not naive when it comes to guys like you, particularly since I used to be a guy like you." Father Sean looked at the pitch setting before loading his token. "Weren't up for a challenge tonight? I think there's some twelve-year-old girls over there hitting faster pitches," he smiled.

"You an expert when it comes to twelve-year-old girls too?" I retorted, borderline offensively.

He pretended to ignore me and turned up the setting. I hoped to watch him embarrass himself. After he connected with the ball multiple times, I realized that was unlikely. He had a beautiful swing.

"You bring me here tonight to show off?" I laughed.

Again, he didn't answer, too focused on swinging. I let him hit a few more, then decided it was only fair that he also have to multitask during his turn in the cage.

"You know, I haven't slept with her yet."

"I figured," he said. The ball and bat made that wonderful cracking sound when he connected.

"Oh, how so?"

"You brought her to the game." He took a moment to briefly look back at me. "You're still trying to impress her." Without missing a beat, he turned back and hit the ball again.

"Well, I probably would've slept with her by now, but Sydney told me the youth center has a policy about staff and volunteers. She said if it became public, Ashland would lose credit for her internship. I figured I could be let go too."

"It's because the center is under the Archdiocese," he explained. "It's to prevent sexual harassment lawsuits." There was that cracking sound again.

"Anyway," I sighed, realizing that nothing was going to wreck the man's concentration, "I don't want to mess anything up for anybody. I figured waiting a month wasn't going to kill me."

"Huh, interesting," he reflected sarcastically. "You're telling me that abstaining from sex is possible...even for someone like you?"

"Yeah, even for someone like me," I confirmed flatly. "I will tell you this though: telling her no is like some sort of aphrodisiac. She was all up on me the other night."

He turned and raised an eyebrow at me, finally letting a pitch go by.

"What?" I asked innocently. "It's the truth. If I had known that's how women responded to a guy withholding, I would've done it a long time ago and saved myself a lot of pleading."

Father Sean returned to his stance.

"You can't tell me you didn't have a similar experience when you returned to pious living, you know, before the collar?" I challenged.

He went back to hitting perfectly but remained silent.

"That's a yes," I laughed, enjoying calling him out. "Don't be mad at me; you're the one who wanted small talk."

"There may have been a few situations," he paused, selecting his words, "when I first returned to trying to follow the Church's teaching...in which similar...reactions from ladies occurred," he admitted before swinging hard and hitting his last pitch. I put my helmet back on and grabbed my bat.

"You want me to turn this all the way down?" he pointed at the pitch setting. "Or we could ask them if they have a tee we could set up for you if you prefer?"

"Leave it," I responded coolly, no stranger to being pulled into a pissing contest.

"Are you going to the Archbishop's gala?" he asked as he walked out of the cage.

"Not that I know of. The Archbishop and I don't tend to hang out socially."

The first pitch whizzed by me.

"The youth center is involved every year. The Archbishop hosts a bunch of donors and nonprofits from the area. The Warrens and the Paulsons will be there. It's two Fridays from now. You should come. I mean, Maura's going to debrief them on how the program went, but I'm sure they'd want to hear from you too."

I finally hit the third pitch. Poorly. "Um, well..."

How was he able to hold a conversation so easily while hitting?

"Come on, man, it'll be fun," he encouraged.

I turned and gave him a doubtful look.

"Well, not fun," he corrected, "but the food's usually pretty good."

"You sure you're not vetting me, Finley?" I swung and missed.

"Yes," he said emphatically. "I would like the program to continue to be funded, and the Warrens and Paulsons seem to like you, therefore it is in the best interest of the program for me to facilitate you being in the same room as them. Relax your left shoulder," he threw in a quick pointer on my swing. I doubted it would help but followed his advice anyway. I shocked myself when I made strong contact with the ball.

"See, I know what I'm talking about," he reasoned. "You could bring Ashland as your date. Impress her even more when she sees you wearing a suit."

"Yes, because wearing a suit and hanging out with the Archbishop is exactly what I need to impress the woman who jumps me every time she's alone with me," I said just after I hit the ball perfectly. He let a silence pass as I waited for my next pitch.

"I'm sure Maura would be happy if you went."

He said it just as the ball was released. I didn't freeze, but the comment wrecked my concentration, and I completely lost my form as I swung. I missed.

"Not that you would care about that," he said nonchalantly when I looked over at him before returning to my stance. "So, the voc-ed program is wrapping up for the year," he commented.

"Yep." I replied quickly, rushing my swing and missing the ball. "Two more meetings."

"You planning on coming back in the fall?"

Up until that moment I hadn't really considered my returning in the fall as a choice. I had been focused on trying to get at least one of the cars drivable within the assigned timeline. Initially, I had planned to have both vehicles fixed, but that had turned out to be too ambitious given the cars that were donated. In the back of my mind, I assumed I would stay until both cars were fixed and that would be that. I paused and focused on only hitting the incoming pitch. Good. Finally, a decent hit.

"Well, the other car in the garage still needs work, so I figured I would stay on until that was done."

"Just asking because I know the Warrens and Paulsons will want to know when you talk to them at the gala."

"Oh, so we've determined that I'm going?" I laughed, thinking of how Maura had described Father Sean's tendency to force people into things.

"I didn't hear you say you weren't going."

Another swing and a miss. And another. And another.

"Should I text Maura and ask her to convince you?" he brought her up again, assuming for some reason she would have some sway on the situation.

"You can, but she's out with her jackass boyfriend tonight." At that moment, I forcefully connected with the ball. My best hit of the night.

"Since when do you have such a strong opinion about who Maura dates?"

"It's not an opinion. It's an observation," I clarified.

Father Sean didn't respond, but I felt the need to explain.

"Do you know what he got her for her birthday?"

Once again, he didn't answer.

"Skis," I exclaimed. "Skis for someone who hates skiing. Now," I hit the ball again, surprising myself with my rhythm, "I don't claim to have the best success at relationships, but even I know that's a jackass move. And since when does Maura like the symphony?" I asked rhetorically, connecting with the ball again. "That's where they are tonight, by the way," I scoffed. "I mean, it's not surprising she wouldn't tell him she has no interest in shit like that, seeing how she turns into a Stepford Wife anytime she's around him, void of any of actual personality or opinion of her own."

I hit the ball five more times, each time with more force than before. I had run out of pitches and stood there catching my breath. Father Sean walked into the cage, maintaining his silence, but giving me a knowing look.

"What?" I asked, wiping some sweat from my brow with the back of my hand. He shrugged, stepping into the batter's box as I stepped aside.

"Just a little surprised to hear you so worked up about a non-factor like Maura," he quoted my description of her from the Mariners game. I rolled my eyes and exited the cage while he asked, "What makes her a non-factor again?"

"I'm not into dating saints."

"You sure it's not that you'd rather get laid than have a meaningful relationship with a woman?"

"I know, shocking. It's crazy how I, and pretty much every other man out there, feel that way."

"About how long does it take you to get bored having sex with a woman?"

"Depends on the sex, depends on the woman."

"But that's how it ends, right? You get bored and move on to the next, probably about two months, no more than three," he stated more so than asked.

"Usually. To be fair though, some of them get bored first."

He hit a couple pitches. I waited for him to make his point.

"And out of all the times you've hung out with Maura, have you ever been bored?"

I didn't answer.

"So," he started loudly and confidently, "you have a woman, and let me clarify: a mentally stable woman, because we both know there will always be those who keep things interesting just by being bat-shit crazy. But anyway, you have a sane woman, who has managed to consistently hold your interest without any sort of promise or expectation of sex."

He had continued to hit perfectly throughout his spiel, which was irritating. He turned to me. "I don't know about you, but I would put my money on life and even sex being the most interesting with her."

I stayed silent.

"You just have to ask yourself if you're mature enough to delay gratification temporarily."

"Well, thank you for that moving sermon, Father Finley," I deflected, "but I'm wise enough to recognize what's unattainable when I see it. And I see no reason to subject myself or Maura to what will ultimately be a train wreck, should I choose to take your advice."

I had lost count of his hits by this point. It was clear Father Sean was just warming up with his first turn.

"Nobility," he laughed. "Always a good disguise for coward-ice. Remember you're talking to the guy who considered marrying her instead of becoming a priest because it was the easier thing to do, not necessarily the right thing."

"Well, I'm starting to wish that had happened so we wouldn't be having this conversation now."

"Sorry," he apologized, again swinging and hitting the ball effortlessly. "I didn't know you approached life the same way you approach the setting on your pitch speed."

"What do you care anyway? I would assume you'd want Maura to be with a puritan like herself, not some heathen who would constantly be trying to get into her pants and disappointing her with his lack of holiness."

"Such low expectations of yourself," he mimicked my comment earlier with a laugh. "Look, Maura can handle a guy who's constantly trying to get into her pants. This, I know. And as for the other part, she doesn't need holiness; she needs faithfulness."

I remained silent and let him finish his pitches, despite not really understanding the difference between the two concepts. I was curious what he meant but thought asking for an explanation would only confirm his suspicions; I cared about Maura more than I was willing to admit, but I still wasn't willing to give up casual sex, regardless of how strong those stupid feelings were starting to become.

MAURA

I sat at my desk finishing up progress notes from the past couple of days. Over three-fourths of my list had been completed; not bad, considering it was only Wednesday.

I crossed another note off my list. Even though it was the end of the day, I decided to stay at the office until my final six notes were recorded.

God, I love crossing things off a list. Is that weird?

Before I could rationalize why it wasn't weird, I heard someone tap on the door. It was Thomas, still wearing his coveralls.

"Hey," I greeted.

"Hey." He cleared his throat. "So, um, we just finished our last day out there."

"I know. Big day. Were they sad?" I waited for a report of some sort of dysfunctional behavior.

"No, not really," he continued to stand in the doorway, "but that's probably because I told them I was coming back in the fall."

"Oh, you are?" I hadn't meant for my voice to sound so surprised. It had crossed my mind that Thomas may not want to continue volunteering his time, but I'd avoided thinking about it because I didn't want to think about how I would no longer see him on a weekly basis. Just as I had avoided thinking about today being his last day.

"Uh, yeah, I mean, we didn't even really get started on the other car so, it just makes sense to stick around until that's finished." He paused. "That is, if you guys decide you want to keep me around."

It wasn't like him to fish for validation.

"Well, you managed not to try to baptize any of the kids or make out with them, so you're doing better than some other volunteers we've had in the past," I said. "Truthfully, we haven't really talked about whether you would come back or not. I think we all hoped you would though."

He nodded, now tapping his knuckles against the doorframe. What else did he want to tell me?

"So, that gala thing this Friday," he began, but then stopped.

I nodded.

"Father Sean suggested that I go in case the donors wanted to talk to me," he said.

I knew it made sense for him to be there, but I couldn't get past Sean, someone who wasn't even part of our staff, taking it upon himself to ask Thomas to be there. Okay, so I hadn't invited Thomas, mostly because I didn't want to see him there with Ashland. The two of them dressed in formal wear, with her internship officially over and there being no need to hold back on any public displays of affection...it was the last thing I wanted to see that evening. I stared at him blankly as thoughts of him making out with Ashland entered my head and left a knot in my stomach.

"Unless you don't think I should go," he said uncertainly.

"No, no," I quickly corrected and forced myself to smile. "Of course. I think that's a great idea. I guess I just thought maybe you wouldn't want to go to something boring like that."

"Well, I'd like to do anything I can to help make sure the program can continue, whether it's for auto-mechanics or some other skill."

He sounded so genuine. Now I felt guilty for being petty. I nodded and there was an awkward silence.

"Father Sean said you were going to give a report about the program. I thought it might be good if I looked it over before Friday?"

"Oh yeah, of course," I confirmed, but didn't offer any dates for when that could happen.

"Do you think maybe I could see it tonight?"

He sounded timid once again. I couldn't blame him for his tone; even I was confused by all my pauses.

"Oh," I attempted to shake myself out of my awkwardness. "Yeah, well," I motioned for him to come into the office and sit down next to my desk.

I closed out of my progress notes and switched over to the report document. "Ann didn't want me printing it out until she had a chance to go over it, but if you have time, you can read it right now. It's about ten pages. But there are some graphs in there, so it's not too long."

"I don't want to keep you here," he backtracked.

"No, it's fine, I was planning to stay later tonight anyway." I turned my computer screen towards him.

"But it's Wednesday. Don't you have Mass?"

"I wasn't planning on going tonight," I said truthfully. I was not in the mood to hang out with the Blessed Sacrament Young Adult crowd on a day that wasn't an obligation, even if my boyfriend was there. Thomas gave me a look of concern.

"Relax, I still go on Sundays," I clarified. "Read away."

He leaned in to get a better look at the report. We sat in silence for a good fifteen minutes. Unfortunately, while Thomas had something to read, I had nothing but my stupid rambling thoughts.

God, he smells good. What is that, aftershave? Why doesn't he smell like gasoline or oil? Is it weird that I'm noticing what he smells like? Probably, yes. Why can't I remember what Ethan smells like?

Finally, Thomas sat back against his chair, signifying that he was done reading.

"Sorry I had to sit here while you read. I know it's awkward, but there are rules about access to my computer," I explained. That was the truth. It was required...I didn't do it because I liked how he smelled.

"Are you going to have to kill me now?" he joked, the first semblance of his personality to appear since he'd arrived.

"Not me. That's Syd's job," I joked back. "So, do you have any questions?"

"Yeah. How was the symphony?" He grinned at his question that had nothing to do with my report.

"It was, uh..."

"That boring, eh?"

"God, yes," I admitted on an exhale. I withheld the fact that the only redeeming quality of the night had been making out in Ethan's car afterwards – very tamely, of course.

"I feel bad. My eyes started to glaze over about half way through. I mean, I feel like I should've liked it. All of those people are really talented. I couldn't do what they were doing, but I just... didn't like it. Guess I'm not cultured."

"With an iPod playlist like yours? I'm shocked you would feel that way," Thomas teased. I reflexively slapped his arm.

"Don't tell Ethan. I told him I loved it. I think he already has plans for us to go to another one. But I think it'll be at Christmas time. That one should be better, right?"

He shrugged.

"I couldn't tell you. We mechanics aren't really the cultured type."

"You're telling me that after living in New York City for four years you didn't become the least bit sophisticated?"

"Hardly. Just pretentious," he clarified. "But I usually reserve that skill for when I go to art galleries. I'll have to show you sometime."

I was caught off guard by his suggestion, especially since he maintained eye contact after saying it.

"Thanks, but I'll let you save that skill for Ashland," I meant for the statement to come across as funny. Too bad it sounded bitter. Attempting to recover, I quickly changed the subject. "So, besides my lack of appreciation for the arts, did you have specific questions about the report?"

"No, it all sounds good. I'm glad that I got to be a part of it," he reflected seriously.

"We are too," I spoke for the center as whole, knowing it would sound too personal to say that I was glad. I wasn't ready to let him leave, so I kept the conversation going. "Hey, how were the batting cages with Sean? Besides him telling you that you have to whore yourself out for donations at the gala." I was proud when I made him smile, a small recovery from my failed Ashland joke.

"Batting cages were fine. Except for the whole part where a priest kicked my ass at hitting."

"I'm guessing Sean failed to tell you that he played for Notre Dame?"

Thomas' mouth opened.

"Son of a bitch. Are you serious? Yes, he failed to share that small fact. Now I'm pissed."

"Finley got you again. I tried to warn you about him," I reminded. "He probably didn't tell you because he thought you wouldn't go with him if you knew. He tends to downplay how athletic he is just so he has someone to play with."

"I take it you were tricked into the batting cages at some point as well?"

"No, not the batting cages, but I remember several horrible dates to the bowling alley and racquetball court."

"Well, we're just going to have find something we're better at than him."

"Good luck." Trying to best Sean at anything had never worked out well for me.

"Just competitive when it comes to trivia about family-friendly films, eh?"

"You gotta stick to your strengths," I said matter-of-factly. I glanced at the clock and hoped he would invite me to dinner like he had done in the past.

"So," he said, noticing that I'd looked at the time, "I should probably get going." He stood up and pulled out his keys, fiddling with them for a bit. "Thanks for letting me see that report. I'll see you Friday night."

"No problem."

Maybe I should invite him to dinner?

I resisted. He probably had plans with Ashland anyway.

"Have a good night."

"You too," he nodded and walked out the door.

It seemed overwhelmingly quiet once Thomas left. What was I going to do over the summer when I had no excuse to talk to him?

Later that night, I was settling into my pathetic dinner of grilled cheese at home when my phone rang. It was my parents. Finally, a break from the silence that had enveloped me since Thomas left my office.

"Hello."

"Hey, kiddo," my dad's voice answered back. "How're you doing?"

"Fine. Just got home from work. Sitting down to a seven-course meal I made from scratch," I kidded.

"Cold cereal?" he guessed knowingly.

"Close, but no. Grilled cheese."

"Wow, stepping it up a bit. Did you use multiple cheeses? Maybe throw a tomato in there?"

"Please, it's impressive I even turned the stove on."

"You want me to send your mother over there to cook you something?" he half joked, but we both knew she'd do it if I asked her to.

"No, I'm good. I think I'll let her have the night off. Did you call just to hear about my riveting dinner plans tonight?"

My dad always had a specific reason for contacting me.

"Well, I just wanted to wish you luck on your big fundraising shin-dig Friday."

"Thanks Dad," I said, still waiting for him to get to his real reason for calling.

He paused a moment.

"So, did you like the symphony? Your mom said you and Ethan went Saturday night."

"It was okay. Kind of slow." This small talk with my dad was starting to feel strange. There was another silence.

"And you really like this Ethan guy?"

There it was: the completely awkward question my dad had been holding back, but the real reason why he'd called.

"Uh…" I paused, unsure of what to say. My dad had made a point never to talk to me about my romantic relationships. He had relied solely on my mom to be his informant all these years. "Yeah…" my voice trailed off. We both knew I didn't want to talk about it, especially with him.

"The only reason I ask is…well, I know things are starting to get kind of serious, and well, Maura…I don't really know how to say this…"

I half expected him to forbid me to go to Vail, which was odd because my parents had never forbidden me from doing anything. They'd never had to.

"You just didn't seem like yourself at dinner and I can't stop thinking about it."

"I wasn't myself?" I feigned cluelessness.

"Yeah, I don't know, you seemed different. I don't know how to pinpoint it, and maybe you were having an off-day, but I just thought I'd call and make sure you're okay."

"Dad, I'm fine. I had a busy day at work and was just tired," I reasoned. So what if it was a lie?

"I figured that might have been it. But I thought I'd call and make sure." Another silence passed. "I know your mother and I joke a lot about wanting you to settle down, but I want you to know that what's most important to us is that you're happy."

"I know, Dad." I pushed away my dinner, no longer hungry.

"It's just that…on your birthday, you didn't really seem happy, and it seemed like Ethan didn't really notice?" His tone had the inflection of a question, like he was seeking confirmation for his observation. "We were surprised he didn't know how much you hate skiing and the snow."

I stayed quiet.

"Maybe you guys are still getting to know each other," he tried to backtrack. "I just want to make sure that as he gets to know you, he knows all of you, because I think you're pretty great. I'd hate for him to miss out on something."

"Thanks, Dad," I managed to get out.

"And if he ends up not liking something about you, he's an idiot."

"Of course," I agreed.

"Okay, well, that's all I really wanted to say."

"Well, thank you."

"All right then. You have a good night," he finished. Clearly, he called me without my mother's knowledge; otherwise she would've insisted on talking to me for the next hour.

"'Okay, you too." I hung up, feeling disappointed in myself.

No matter how much I tried to be the serious, devout Catholic woman I presented to Ethan, it was obvious to everyone else in my life that I could never be that person.

THOMAS

I waited at the entrance of Ashland's apartment building, feeling overdressed and out of place, since her building housed mostly college students. Ashland came out the front door and stood before me, wearing a strapless beige dress that landed just above her knee. She looked amazing, but it was a fairly risqué fashion choice for an event with a bunch of religious people. The dress was the same color as her skin and hugged every wonderful curve she had.

"Hello," I greeted, as she pressed herself up against me.

"Hey." She placed both her hands against my chest, just as she had done the first time she kissed me. "So, technically, I'm not an intern anymore. You sure you don't want to come upstairs before we go to this thing?" She stared at me intently.

If it had been six months ago I would have said yes without hesitation, but now I declined. "I don't like being rushed, and I don't want to be late."

The thought of finally sleeping with Ashland had been on my mind all week, but with the distinct plan of doing it after the gala. I worried that if I slept with her before I would feel guilty and it would stick with me all night, throwing off my likability factor and negatively affecting potential donations. That wasn't logical, but compartmentalizing felt right. For a few hours I could be good, volunteer Thomas; the one that hung out with a priest in his free time. After the gala, I could go back to being slacker, asshole Thomas – the one who only thought about getting laid.

"Fair enough," Ashland said in a pout before kissing me, long and hard. She broke away, proud of the dumbfounded look on my face.

"Let's go get this over with," she sighed, walking towards the street. "Where's your truck?" She turned to me.

"I thought I'd class it up tonight," I answered, clicking the key to unlock the sedan.

"I miss the truck and the coveralls." She opened her own door and got in.

I attempted to make small talk during the drive. Ashland didn't seem interested in maintaining any sort of conversation, providing one-word answers throughout the exchange and half-hearted shrugs. She could have been upset because I turned her down again when I picked her up.

Once I handed over the keys to the valet, I placed my hand on the small of her back as we walked into the lobby.

"Is something wrong?" I asked quietly.

"It's fine. I'm just kind of burnt out."

"With what?"

"The youth center," she said as if it were obvious. "I'll be glad when this night is over, for various reasons, of course." She gave me a half smile.

"You didn't like working there? I thought you liked it. When we went out you said you were interested in working with the homeless."

I was confused. I had always thought she enjoyed her time there. I didn't have a miserable time when I was there, so I guess I assumed we had the same experience. Although, I was probably held to a lower standard of responsibility than a graduate intern.

"I do like working with the homeless, just not under the rule of an archaic, sexist, homophobic dictatorship," Ashland said bluntly as we walked into the ballroom.

"Thomas!" Father Sean exclaimed the moment we entered. I saw Ashland paste a smile on her face before I greeted him.

I held out my hand and shook his.

"Hey," he nodded and then turned to Ashland.

"Ashland, nice to see you again." He shook her hand too. "Good to see you guys found the place all right. People are already asking a lot of questions about the youth center, so it's great you guys are here. I keep trying to talk to them about Newman, but it doesn't seem to be holding anybody's interest," he said happily.

Just then someone called over to him. "I think Maura and Sydney are over that way," he pointed to the other corner of the room. "I'll catch up with you guys in a little bit."

Briefly forgetting what Ashland had shared when we walked in, I decided to go find Maura. I headed over to the corner of the ballroom. It didn't register that Ashland had grabbed my hand until I was about half way there. I guess we no longer had to hide our involvement with one another.

I saw Maura before she saw me. She was wearing the dark blue dress I had seen laid out on her bed from the other night. She looked beautiful in it, just like I expected she would. However, what I noticed most was how she was smiling. Maura smiled more than any other person I had ever met, but tonight she was beaming.

"Hey, Thomas, Ashland, you made it," Sydney greeted, calling my attention away from Maura.

"This is Thomas O'Hollaren," Maura introduced me to the strangers on her left. "He's our volunteer voc-ed instructor. And this is Ashland Andersen; she just finished up her first-year internship with us. Thomas, Ashland, this is Bill and Jeanette Dawson and John and Mary Stewart; they've been donating to the youth center for over ten years now."

I reached out and shook their hands. Ashland just nodded.

"We are so excited to hear about the vocational training that you've been able to provide," John said.

"I've really enjoyed being part of it."

"And what are the specific skills you've been able to teach?" Jeanette asked.

"Basic maintenance skills: changing oil, flushing transmission fluid, alignment, things like that."

"In addition, though," Maura added, "they helped rebuild an engine and replace a radiator," she looked to me to confirm. I nodded, glad that Sydney had pulled Ashland into a side conversation so I didn't have to worry about her becoming any more bored than she already looked.

"It was great," Maura continued. "Sydney and I got to sit in every week, and it was just amazing to see that group of teens become so focused. The most common feedback we got was how accomplished they felt because of it. One of the kids even said to me, 'You know, I've never been good at school, but now I know I can do this. And that means things will be okay.'"

The group was captivated by Maura as she shared more about the experience of sitting in on the instruction. Admittedly, I found myself captivated as well by her passion. It probably didn't hurt that she was wearing that dress.

"So, you own a shop here in Seattle?" One of the strangers pulled me out of my rapt attention before my stare could be considered ogling.

"Yes. O'Hollaren's Auto, in Queen Anne. My brother and I own it."

They proceeded to ask me various questions about the shop and being a mechanic that I knew no one else there was interested in. I recognized that my involvement with the youth center would ultimately be good for business, given the potential for racking up new clientele at events like this one. I had anticipated this when they initially asked me to participate, but now I felt guilty that my reasons for getting involved might have been more opportunistic than altruistic.

"Well," Jeanette gently touched Maura's arm, "we'd better get around to talking to some of these other nonprofits like the Archbishop intended, but you know you'll always be our favorite," she whispered loudly. She and Maura shared a laugh.

"Be sure you send any folks who don't know about us our way," Maura instructed with a smile as the group moved on.

Maura's hair was intricately styled, with French braids on the side, forming a low twisted bun in the back. Why I noticed and appreciated this, I had no fucking clue.

"So, Maura, you seem to be having a good time," I commented.

"Of course," Sydney responded. "She's talking about people to other people...and they're all Catholic. It's like Christmas day to her."

"I would be just as happy if the people we were talking to weren't Catholic," Maura said matter-of-factly. Sydney gave her a doubtful look.

"And how many references to Saint Anthony have you made already tonight?"

"Three," Maura muttered.

"Three. And we haven't even been here an hour yet."

"That's only because people kept misplacing things when we first got here. He's the patron saint of lost items—"

"For Catholics," Sydney finished Maura's sentence, confirming her point.

"I don't think he discriminates when it comes to helping people find their shit. And I will remind you of that the next time you lose your keys," Maura said good-naturedly.

Just when I had gladly forgotten that he would probably be there, Ethan walked up holding two glasses of wine.

"Here you go," he said, handing one to Maura.

She smiled, thanking him and taking a sip. Great. It was time for her to turn into a shell of herself now that he had joined us.

"Hey, Thomas. Good to see you." He shook my hand firmly, then looked over at Ashland. "Hi, I'm Ethan, Maura's boyfriend."

"Ashland," she said simply, briefly shaking his hand. She then returned to appearing like she couldn't care less about the conversation.

"Julie finally got here from work," Sydney announced, looking at her phone. "I'm going to go meet her out front. You guys should grab some food," she suggested to Ashland and me before leaving.

"We already sufficiently stuffed ourselves before everyone else got here," Maura informed. "They have wait staff walking around with trays, but there's also a station over there. It's pretty fancy. There's like, three different types of meatballs."

I was amused by her review of the catering. I turned to Ashland.

"I'm not really hungry," she said, unimpressed by the promise of various meatballs. It seemed weird to walk away and leave her there with Maura and Ethan to get food for myself. I decided to wait it out until someone walked by with a tray.

"What about a drink?" I offered, thinking she probably wouldn't turn down free alcohol.

"Wine sounds great," she said with the same enthusiasm as saying she wasn't hungry. I started to move towards the bar.

"No," she stopped me. "I'll go get it for us," she smiled and kissed me on the cheek before walking away.

"I didn't realize you had a girlfriend, Thomas," Ethan said when she was out of earshot.

"Yeah, uh, not really at that stage yet," I corrected.

He nodded. Maura took a sip of wine, trying to tolerate the silence. I knew she was racking her brain for something that all of us could talk about. We were probably seconds away from her asking us what our favorite fruit was. To avoid that, I decided to play nice with Ethan, at least for the night. "So, any vacations planned for the summer?"

"Well, I go down to an orphanage in Mexico every July." He looked over at Maura while touching the small of her back. "I'm hoping Maura decides to join me. But she hasn't seemed to want to commit just yet."

"Helping poor kids as a vacation. That does sound like it's right up your alley, Maura," I teased.

"I told you, I have to talk to my boss," she reminded Ethan patiently. "I think this summer is going to be pretty busy, especially since Sydney's going to Europe for two weeks at the end of July."

She really didn't want to go, but I don't think Ethan could tell. That confused me, especially since spending time at an orphanage seemed to be way more in line with her interests than skiing or the symphony. If I had liked Ethan, I might have felt sorry for him.

"She's so committed to those kids she works with," Ethan said to me proudly. "Sometimes I think she forgets there's a lot of other kids outside of Seattle who could use her help."

Complimenting followed quickly by guilting was an interesting tactic to use. Thankfully, Ashland returned with our wine because I didn't know how to respond. Sydney returned with Julie shortly after. Sydney quickly reintroduced Julie to Ashland and me, and then introduced her to Ethan. When Julie let go of shaking Ethan's hand, Maura's mouth dropped open and she quickly snatched up Julie's hand. She held it up, displaying what appeared to be an engagement ring.

"Oh my God! Shut up!" Maura exclaimed loudly with a grin. "What? What? When? Ahhh!" Maura couldn't seem to form a complete sentence in between exclaiming with giddiness and bouncing up and down, all while still holding Julie's hand. Finally, she let go and wrapped her arms around both Sydney and Julie. "I'm so happy for you!"

"Easy, easy," Sydney instructed calmly. "Play it cool."

Maura gave her a pointed look, communicating that it was unreasonable for Sydney to expect that from her.

"Congratulations," Ashland said, appearing finally interested in something going on that night.

"Thanks," Sydney said.

"I can't believe you didn't say anything!" Maura exclaimed

"Gee, I don't know why I didn't, seeing as how calm and collected you are right now."

Maura glared at Sydney. "Whatever. You wanted this reaction. You knew this reaction was inevitable. If you didn't want this reaction, you would've told me about it earlier," she argued.

Sydney finally let out a mischievous grin. "Yeah, maybe," she admitted.

Maura shook her head and waited for an explanation. "So when and how did it happen?" The half-confession from Sydney seemed to be enough to restore Maura's initial excitement.

"Yesterday, we were sitting at dinner," Julie began the story. "I asked Syd if she wanted anything in particular for her birthday, because it's coming up, and she said she had been thinking about it for a really long time and that the one thing she wanted was for me to be her fiancée, and then she pulled out the ring."

"I've been walking around with it on me like an idiot for like five weeks, waiting for the right time," Sydney confessed.

"Oh," Maura's eyes began to tear up. She held both her hands to her chest. "That's just the sweetest thing! And you said you weren't the romantic type," she accused, shoving Sydney.

I loved watching just how many emotions Maura was cycling through throughout this exchange.

"What can I say? Jules brings it out of me."

I glanced over at Ethan, who had remained silent. He was expressionless. Was this his first time realizing Maura's best friend was gay? I was surprised his presence didn't cause Maura to hold back her excitement for Sydney and Julie. It was a welcomed change from how stifled she always acted around him.

"Oh my gosh," Maura realized, "you are going to have so much fun planning the wedding, Julie! Do you have a date? Do you want it to be in the spring or summer? What're your colors going to be? You're going to wear a dress, right?"

"Whoa, whoa, whoa." Sydney held up a hand, signaling for Maura to calm down. Julie appeared to be just as entertained by Maura and Sydney's exchange as I was. "It's been a day. Give us a minute, will you? I mean, we at least need to start by deciding who will be in the wedding party."

Maura sighed.

Sydney paused for a moment. "Maura, I was wondering if you would like to be my best person?"

Maura's eyes grew wide. "Are you serious?"

Sydney nodded.

Predictably, Maura's eyes teared up again. She touched her hand over her heart. "Aww, you guys, thank you, of course." She pulled Sydney and Julie into another hug, much to Sydney's dismay, but she tolerated it. Maura pulled back, wiping her eyes.

"I'm the best person! Yay!" she exclaimed quietly one more time, gently clapping her hands together.

Sydney sighed and shook her head, but still smiled.

"Well, now that we got that over with," Sydney said in a labored tone. "Ashland, on my way back in with Jules, I ran into some managers I know from a housing agency. They are always looking for interns. I said I would bring you back over to them and introduce you. I'll work this side," she said to Maura while she, Julie, and Ashland walked away.

Father Sean stopped to say hello to Sydney and shake Julie's hand as he approached us. He looked like a campaigning politician; his grin never wavered.

"Hey guys," he greeted, patting my back. "Having a good time?"

We all nodded.

"Father Lorenzo from Saint Peter's has some parishioners he wants to introduce you to," he said to Maura. "And I was wondering if I could borrow this guy for a second?"

"Oh, has his fan club showed up?" I assumed Maura was refer-ring to the Warrens and Paulsons.

"Actually, I was going to introduce him to the Archbishop," he informed.

Maura let out a laugh. "What? Really? The Archbishop? That's a good move, Father Finley. I'm impressed."

"What?" He maintained his look of innocence.

Maura glanced at me, realizing I needed more explanation.

"Father Finley, here, is making sure that the Archbishop, who has a background in homeless ministry and is particularly fond of our program, knows just how involved he was in helping set up our voc-ed program. Father Finley has to make sure the Archbishop meets the very mechanic he convinced to come help the children for free. What, Sean? Does Newman need a new roof? Are you already thinking of expanding the seating area? Is it finally time for those stained-glass windows? You're certainly an ambitious first year director."

I was still lost. Father Sean remained cool, not flustered by her pointed tone.

"If those things were needed, Maura, I'm sure the Western Dominican Province and the Archdiocese would hold a meeting and determine an appropriate way to secure funds, as opposed to me relying on the Archbishop's favor like you're suggesting. You know, not everything is politics."

The dots started to connect for me.

"Sorry, Father, but you must have forgotten that I've worked in the nonprofit sector for five years. Everything is politics," she said knowingly, taking a sip of her wine.

"Did you get that line from watching The West Wing or House of Cards?" he joked, deflecting her accusation. "This one," he pointed at her, looking at Ethan and then over at me, "was obsessed with West Wing reruns when we dated. You put Ethan through that torture too?"

"Yes, because watching an award-winning TV series is torture compared to having to watch all five Die Hard movies," she snapped back. He'd managed to hook and distract her from her original point. It was impressive that he did it with such ease.

"Well, I think it's clear which one has more cultural merit," he said obviously, now smiling at his effect on her. "Ethan, how many seasons has she forced you to watch so far?"

"Uh, none. I'm not really into TV or movies, so I guess she's decided to spare me. Honestly, it's surprising to hear that Maura would even care about watching something that had anything to do with politics. She's so neutral when it comes to that stuff."

"Well, I guess you're the lucky one," he said to Ethan while looking at Maura. Those two seemed to have an entire language when it came to the looks they exchanged with one another.

"So, Thomas, what do you say? Let's go say hi to the Archbishop," he motioned with his head.

"Sounds good. I'm sure he'd love to hear about how you used to play baseball for the Irish," I called him out, for Maura. "Or were you planning on hustling him at the batting cages like you did me?"

He paused, realizing he'd been caught.

"Aw man, she told you that?" He laughed nervously. "I was a walk-on. I mean, that hardly counts," he justified.

"Fair point," Maura chimed in. "I mean, Rudy was a walk-on and it's not like he mattered enough for them to make a movie about him or anything."

Father Sean stared at her.

"You do remember the movie Rudy? That's the one where you cry like a little baby every time you watch it." She had found her retaliation.

"It's called having a heart. You're the weird one for not crying at the end of Rudy," he argued.

"All I'm saying is, maybe it would have been a better message if he found something else that he was really good at doing."

Father Sean threw his head back with a heavy sigh. They'd had this debate before. The glint in her eye told me that she knew she was going to get that exact reaction from him.

"That was the whole point of the story," he exclaimed. "He was good at inspiring people because he didn't give up."

Maura nodded, communicating more placation than agreement.

"Thomas, Ethan, come on, you guys gotta help me out here." Father Sean looked expectantly at me. While, I did agree with him, I continued to align myself with Maura.

"You know, it's been awhile since I've seen it," I said. "To be fair to both of your arguments, I feel like I would have to watch it again. That is, of course, if I can get over the fact that my last experience with a Notre Dame alumnus was one of deception."

"You want to meet the Archbishop, or not?" he asked shortly, realizing I would not take his side.

Ann called to Maura, motioning her over to another cluster of people. Maura excused herself from myself and Father Sean, grabbed Ethan's hand, and went to join the other group. I watched her walk away.

"That's a considerable amount of time to stare at someone you're not interested in."

I rolled my eyes.

"I never said she wasn't nice to look at."

"True," he granted. "Let's get a drink before we meet up with Archbishop Bennett."

"I'm going to need some food first." My mother would kill me if I met the Archbishop while tipsy.

"All right then." He directed me toward the serving station where I eagerly grabbed a plate and loaded up on appetizers, most them involving bacon in some way.

"It's clear this isn't a Jewish event," I joked.

"There's a reason why the majority of fundraising is done after Lent. For some reason, people don't enjoy it as much when you serve them soup and skimp on the wine."

I was consumed with eating while Father Sean talked to various people who walked by. He seemed to know everybody.

"Come on," he said when I had devoured everything on my plate, leading me over to the bar to get some wine.

"Can I ask you something?" I asked before I took a sip. "Was there any truth to what Maura said? About the whole politics thing?"

He shrugged. "To an extent, yeah," he answered honestly. "But I like to think I'm not as conniving as she makes me out to be. What I said at the cages was true; I would like the voc-ed program to continue and in order to do that I have to make sure the Warrens and Paulsons approve of what's being done with their money. Additionally, they are my largest donors at the Newman Center, and keeping them happy, in general, is in the best interest of the Newman Center.

"Now, the other side," he continued, "is that Newman also has to depend on the financial support of the Archdiocese, because college students don't tithe. So, it's vital to keep the Archbishop happy. I knew the minute I took over at Newman that we needed to be more involved in the youth center, not just because it's a good community program, but also because it would please Archbishop Bennett.

"When the Warrens and the Paulsons came to me saying they had a large amount of money they wanted to go towards a social justice program, it was beneficial to direct it towards the youth center rather than attempting to develop something on my own. It's relatively the same thing as the positive publicity your shop gets from you volunteering your time. Is that the only reason you do it? No, probably not. But are you going to turn down any business it generates?" he asked rhetorically and then took a drink, wrapping up his explanation. "Hopefully you're not too jaded now."

"No," I said. His savvy was commendable. "But why does it piss Maura off so much?"

"She doesn't like playing the whole game," he said. "In her eyes, people, religious institutions, and the government should be putting their money towards programs like the youth center because it's the right thing to do, not because they like the people who told them to put their money towards it."

"She looks like she doesn't mind it so much tonight," I countered.

"I said she didn't like playing the game; I didn't say she couldn't do it, and do it very well, I might add. She was charming enough to get you to volunteer."

"You make that sound like an impressive feat," I laughed, but knew it was true.

"Some women have a way of inspiring us to live up to our potential, especially when they're nice to look at."

I sighed and shook my head, a common response to Father Sean at this point.

"I see what you're trying to do."

He took a drink of his wine, not denying anything.

"But I hate to break it to you that I plan on leaving tonight with another woman."

"And how fulfilling do you think that will be?" he challenged.

"Ah, Father Sean, I think we both know the answer to that question, but I understand your confusion, being six years out." I patted his back, purposely avoiding his question altogether. "Come on, let's go meet that Archbishop before they all figure out what a heathen I am."

I hated to admit it, but I truly enjoyed the rest of the evening. Father Sean and I played off each other well. The Archbishop seemed impressed with the work that had been done at the youth center. He even mentioned sending his car to our shop the next time it needed to be serviced, which I knew would leave Michael on cloud nine, should it ever happen. Father Sean introduced me to a few other donors, and when our conversations concluded, they made their way over to Ann and pulled out their checkbooks.

As cheesy as it was, I felt good participating in the whole night, knowing I was helping kids like Juan and Justin get more support for their future. I was having such a good time basking in the joy of my newfound humanitarianism, I had completely forgotten about Ashland and where she was. In the middle of a conversation with two middle-aged women, who were clearly relishing the attention they were receiving from Father Sean and me, I felt a tap on my shoulder. I turned around to see Ashland.

"Hey, I've been looking for you," she said quietly before leaning in to whisper in my ear, "I'm ready to rip that suit off of you."

Okay, so that was a turn on. I managed to maintain my cool though.

"Sure, just one second," I said, turning back to the ladies and Father Sean. "I'm sorry, but I have to get my date home."

"Oh, and all this time, I thought I was your date," one of the women lamented playfully.

"Next time, next time," I joked back. "Ladies, you have my card. Let me know if you have any more questions or even if you have some concerns about your cars. Have a good night. Make sure you keep Father Sean out of trouble," I instructed before making my exit with Ashland.

I briefly considered finding Maura to say goodbye, but I had a hunch Ashland didn't have any patience left. Once we were driving away from the hotel, Ashland let out a heavy sigh.

"Well, I'm glad that's over," she announced. "You looked like you had a good time with Father What-A-Waste and the bourgeois fan club." She ran her fingers through my hair.

"What can I say? Get a little red wine in me and I'll ask anybody to donate money for the kids."

"Ugh, the whole thing is disgusting. Just thinking about how much money all those people have and what little amount of it they give, and yet they still feel good about themselves..."

It still seemed a little arrogant to scoff at any amount of donation just because she believed someone was in the position to give more. In my opinion, that level of judgment was above my moral standing, especially when I'd seen some people write out checks in the thousands that night.

"It's like they don't even really care about fixing any of the problems," she continued. "They just want a warm fuzzy feeling and to pretend that they have a clear conscience. You know?"

She looked to me for agreement. Not wanting to debate, I tried to find a neutral way out. It didn't seem right to critique a bunch of people I didn't know, who spent their evening giving money to charitable causes.

"You know, I hadn't thought much about what they were getting out of it. I'm just glad that the voc-ed program can continue and potentially expand someday."

"Aww, it really is commendable how much you love working with those kids."

Despite the condescension, I was hopeful things had gotten back on track. I wanted Ashland to go back to being the woman I wanted to sleep with instead of the overly-critical grad student who had shown up as my date that night.

"So, I'm wondering why that priest always wants to hang out with you? Is he trying to get you to become a priest too?"

"No," I laughed at the absurdity of the question.

"Are you sure? Maybe he has a crush on you and wants you to become a priest so he can be with you." Her tone was only half joking.

I gave her a look that said I thought her comment was even more bizarre than her question.

"What?" she laughed. "Oh, you know odds are he's probably gay and, like, super in denial about it. I mean, really, think about it. It's either that or he's just incredibly weird. I mean, can you think of any priest you've ever heard of that was normal?"

I didn't say anything, not really wanting to dignify any of her statements with a response.

"Oh, come on, Thomas, you know I'm right."

"I haven't really met a whole lot of people in general who I thought were normal," I answered. "And if he were gay, it wouldn't make sense to recruit a guy you were interested in because it would make the whole celibacy thing a lot more challenging."

"Oh, yeah right. You really think he doesn't have sex? You've got to be kidding me," she laughed with disbelief.

I exited the freeway and headed towards her apartment. "It's not really a concern of mine if Father Sean is having sex or not."

For the first time, I wished she would stop sharing her thoughts.

"The whole Catholic organization is just so deplorable with its hypocrisy and oppression. I mean, they want to sit there and pretend like nobody should have sex, yet they want everybody to have a million babies. And of course, they won't let any woman think for herself and have the right to do what she wants to do with her own body. I guess I can understand why men could easily be part of that religion, since they have all the power, but why any woman would willingly partake and raise her own children in it is beyond me. Seriously, they have to be either incredibly dimwitted or in some sort of abusive situation."

I pulled up to her apartment and parked. Her last sentence triggered something inside of me.

"You realize my entire family is Catholic, right?" I tried to keep my tone informative, but the words came out more emotional than I wanted. It was probably the implication that every female in my family, specifically my mother, was either stupid or abused by their spouse.

She paused for a moment, taken aback by my response. "Well, no, but you said you weren't religious."

"I'm not, but–"

"So, obviously, you see the flaws I'm talking about, especially if you decided to stop being Catholic."

I shook my head, irritated by how she was generalizing everything.

"That's not how it is. I didn't just stop being Catholic; that's not how it works."

"So then how does it work? It seems pretty simple to me; you either subscribe to a religion or not."

"What I subscribe to isn't the point," I tried to get away from having to define exactly what I believed.

"Then what is the point, Thomas?"

I paused, trying to sound rational and not defensive. "The point is, it's narrow-minded to say that all priests are weird or all Catholic women are stupid. It's just not true."

"So you're telling me that you're okay with those people wanting to outlaw abortion and birth control and gay marriage? Because I think that's pretty narrow-minded," she replied sharply.

"Not everyone who's Catholic thinks that way."

"Well then they shouldn't be Catholic," she fired back.

"That's not how it works," I said again, knowing it was a poor response.

"You keep saying that, so then why don't you tell me how it works?" she challenged.

"I don't know," I admitted with a sigh, rubbing my forehead. "I don't know how it works." She looked at me expectantly.

"I just know that there's more to it than what you're saying, and there's too much good that comes from it to completely write it off as an institution that only causes harm."

We sat in silence for a moment. I looked over at her and something felt different, even though she looked exactly the same. There was no desire to sleep with her anymore, not after knowing everything she had just shared.

It was the first time that knowing a woman's opinion about something had prevented me from wanting to sleep with her. I couldn't think of a time when there was ever a woman as good-looking and as willing as Ashland when I'd let anything get in the way of having sex with her, especially for the first time. Sleeping with her was probably always going to be a pointless endeavor with no real meaning beyond momentary physical gratification...so why she had suddenly dropped below some sort of standard that I didn't even know I had until that moment was lost on me. But the fact remained; it just wasn't worth it anymore.

"Well, I didn't really expect to have such a heavy discussion tonight," she softened her tone. "How about we go upstairs and you finally let me take advantage of you."

She unfastened her seatbelt and leaned towards me. I stared forward, part of me wanting to turn her down before she made contact with me, the other part wanting to not care, like I had done so easily with women in the past.

"I think I'm just going to go home." It came out half-heartedly, not enough to stop her advance. She began kissing my neck and moved up to my ear.

"You know, there's really no point in playing hard to get anymore," she whispered.

I kept my hands on the steering wheel, desperately wanting to be strong enough not to give in. A voice in the back of my mind rationalized that she didn't care about the difference in opinion, so there was no reason for me to let it get in the way of something that was going to feel so good.

"Ashland, I don't think this is going to work out," I announced, glad that there was finally conviction in my voice. She backed away and stared me down.

"What?" The confusion was evident in her voice. "You don't think what? All because I spoke my mind about a fucked-up church and belief system that you said you didn't even care about before?" she raised her voice.

"I never said that," I argued quietly.

"You clearly gave me that impression. I can't believe you had me wait a whole fucking month for this," she laughed with disbelief. "You know what? No, it's fine, I really would probably regret sleeping with a misogynistic, homophobic, hypocritical asshole. So thank you for sparing me."

She got out and promptly slammed the door before storming into her building. I sat there for a moment, her final words replaying in my head. I felt shitty, but thankful I wasn't going to have one more thing in my life to regret.

MAURA

It was a little after eleven thirty and the gala was coming to an end, with only a few lingering guests left in the ballroom. I volunteered to be the last of our staff to leave the event. Before I went to search for Ethan, who I had lost track of earlier, I stopped by the bar to get one last glass of wine. It was only my second of the evening. Fundraising had left me preoccupied. I was savoring my first taste when I heard Sean's voice.

"Always a good idea to score as much free booze as possible," he said, joining me.

"Is that what you're teaching the college kids?"

"So, how did the youth center fare tonight? It looked like there were a lot people talking to you," he observed.

"I was killing it tonight," I proclaimed proudly.

"You usually do. Maybe we can get you to be in charge of fundraising for Newman."

"Oh, and take all the fun away from you? Sorry, homeless teens are a slightly easier sell than a church serving mostly privileged college kids." I took a drink.

"So, where's your date?" Sean asked, glancing around the bar area.

"I don't know. He wandered off to talk to some priest from Mercer Island about three hours ago. Knowing my luck, he's probably halfway to the seminary by now."

"Would you feel lucky if that happened?" He attempted to ask the question nonchalantly, but I knew he was dredging up our last one-on-one conversation.

"Not half as lucky as I felt when you left," I answered smartly, not even bothering to look at him when I replied. He wasn't going to wreck my good mood; not tonight.

Ethan walked back into the ballroom and looked around before spotting Sean and me. He didn't smile when we made eye contact.

"You must be pretty proud of this lady tonight," Sean said to him once he stood before us.

Ethan raised his brow.

"She was inspiring a lot of generosity tonight," Sean clarified.

"Are you ready to go?" Ethan turned to me, not acknowledging Sean's comment. This was the coldest I'd ever seen him act. My smile disappeared for the first time that night.

"Uh, sure," I responded quietly, putting my glass down on a nearby table. "Have a good night, Sean."

Ethan barely nodded goodbye.

We walked in silence out of the hotel and continued to stand that way as the valet retrieved his car. He hadn't touched me since returning. Ethan being upset was foreign territory to me. I tested the waters.

"Did you have a good conversation with Father Henderson?" I asked once we were settled in the car and on our way home. He was probably frustrated that I had stayed so late and didn't pay very much attention to him throughout the night. Right?

"Yeah, it was fine," he was curt.

More silence followed. I could not stand it when I knew some-one was mad at me but refused to provide any sort of information why. Not giving him enough attention seemed to be the most log-ical guess.

"I'm sorry I didn't spend more time with you tonight." As usual, I wanted to avoid arguing altogether, so I skipped ahead to apologizing.

Maybe I should explain why I wasn't able to spend very much time with him...but he may not accept the reason...and we would end up arguing.

"It's fine, Maura. I knew you were working. I didn't expect very much attention tonight." His tone was even. There was still tension though – and more silence. If I tried hard enough, I could wait out the silence. After five minutes, which felt like an hour, I couldn't.

"Is something wrong?" I finally asked.

He shook his head, like he expected me to know the answer to my own question. We exited the freeway. I looked at him expec-tantly, hoping my stare would somehow force him to talk. He let out a heavy sigh, taking a moment to consider whether he should tell me or not.

"At what point were you going to tell me you are in favor of gay marriage?"

I stayed quiet. It was pointless to act like I hadn't hidden it from him.

When I didn't respond, Ethan continued. "I felt like I didn't even know who you were tonight."

I waited for him to say something else; this time the silence didn't bother me.

"Maura, you have to respond," he said firmly.

"Is it such a big deal if I'm okay with a secular government providing marriage equality for everyone? No one's saying the Catholic Church, or any church for that matter, has to provide it." I deflected from my deception.

"Maura, it's blatantly against Church teaching. Are you okay with a secular government letting people marry farm animals too?"

Okay, now I was annoyed.

"Why is it you people always go right to comparing being gay to bestiality? It's offensive and obviously not the same thing," I raised my voice. No point in censoring myself anymore.

"What do you mean 'you people'? You mean Catholics? Like what you claim to be?" he raised his voice back.

"No, people who oppose gay marriage. We live in a pluralistic society. We can't force people to live like Catholics or any other religion when they're not. Otherwise none of us would ever get to eat bacon." So it wasn't the best point, but it was the first one that came out of my mouth.

"You really want to reduce this to a joke?"

"Fine," I declared. "You want me to be serious? Do you understand how overrepresented gay and transgender teens are in the homeless population? Forty percent! That's a ridiculous number. It's because they get kicked out of their homes. Usually by their own family. And given the higher risk for violence against them, they can't even access most resources for fear of being beaten, possibly to death. They are four times more likely to commit suicide," I could've gone on with more statistics, but he interrupted me.

"Maura, that's unfortunate, but it has nothing to do with you agreeing with something that clearly goes against the Catechism."

"Marriage represents an idea of a future to so many people beyond any religious affiliation, a hope that they can have a family, a happy ending. The fact that the government came out and recognized that it wasn't right to discriminate against who gets to participate in that anymore sends a huge message to those kids. It validates them and who they are."

"So, this is who you are? Someone who thinks validating people is more important than morality? Care to tell me your thoughts on abortion?" He paused briefly but didn't really give me a chance to answer. "On second thought, I don't think I can handle it right now," he assumed the worst of me.

We made it to my building. He took a deep breath and turned to look at me. "Why? Maura, why were you keeping all of this from me?"

"Because I knew you were going to react this way."

"So you just thought you wouldn't say anything and hope I wouldn't notice when you took me as your date to Sydney's wedding?"

"Well, obviously I wasn't going to take you to the wedding. I'm not stupid," I muttered.

He continued to stare at me, expecting more of an explanation. He had every right to be frustrated with me.

"You just seemed to like me so much, at least who you thought I was...and I just thought...maybe I should try to be that person... because..."

"Because?"

"I don't know...it was what I was supposed to do if I wanted to marry a Catholic." It sounded senseless when I said it aloud.

"Maura, do you love me?"

"I think so."

"You think so?" he scoffed. This, of course, would be the one time he expected me to be more passionate.

"I've been so worried that if you found out the way I thought about some things...you wouldn't want to be with me anymore," I paused. "But it never seemed like you really cared to know what I thought anyway," I offered my only defense quietly.

Ethan didn't respond and when the silence stretched out I started to wonder whether he was just waiting for me to get out of the car.

"Well, I'm glad I found out now versus later," he finally spoke.

I just sat there, waiting for him to tell me what was going to happen.

"This isn't going to work out." he sounded disappointed, but I thought he gave up pretty quickly for someone who had said he loved me only hours ago. Evidently, he thought my newly discovered flaws were irredeemable. Guess I wasn't worth fighting for.

"I'm sorry," I said reflexively. I knew I wasn't really all that sorry.

"Maura, there's no need to be sorry," he said, logical as ever. "Maybe, next time though, be a little bit more honest about who you are and what you want."

I wanted to tell him that life was more complicated than just following what was written in the Catechism. I wanted to tell him that loving someone meant actually taking time to learn and appreciate what someone believed rather than rejecting them at the first sign of disagreement. And I really, really, really wanted to tell him that skiing was stupid. But I didn't. It was a waste of time, just like our relationship.

Instead, I simply nodded and let myself out of the car to head back to my apartment, failing once again to be the person somebody wanted.

MAURA

The break-up with Ethan hit me harder than I thought it would, even though I wasn't shocked by it at all. Deep down I knew it would be over the minute he met Sydney and started to really understand my worldview. It was ridiculous how long I had been able to keep the wool pulled over his eyes – and my own – trying to convince us both that we could be right for each other.

At least now that the relationship was over, I was less anxious. Constantly trying to be Catholic enough for Ethan had been draining. But stress relief aside, the confirmation that I was a subpar mate in the world of Catholic dating was what seemed to resonate – and hurt – the most.

Ethan seemed to pick himself back up without any sort of problem; I saw him sitting next to Jessica at Mass two days after we broke up. He even hugged her during the sign of peace. Perhaps it's easier to rebound when you know that the person you were dating was a fraud and is probably going to hell for voting for too many Democrats. I had no doubt that he was praying for my misguided soul. You know, when he wasn't busy not making out with her.

It was somewhat masochistic for me to continue going to the eleven o'clock Mass when I knew Ethan would be there. A healthier person would have switched Mass times, but I reasoned that it would have been a sign of weakness to avoid him. Additionally, I didn't want him assuming that I had stopped attending altogether, giving him any more reason to believe that I wasn't a "real" Catholic.

However, after three weeks of feeling like no one in the young adult group acknowledged that I was even there, I concluded that in the separation, Ethan had gotten custody of the eleven o'clock Sunday Mass and the Wednesday evening Mass. Apparently it wasn't just the Amish who were into shunning.

God, I can't believe I probably would've said yes if he'd actually asked me to marry him.

This thought had been popping into my head routinely since the breakup. It was ridiculous how much I had been willing to overlook just because Ethan was devout and decent looking. While I was relieved, that feeling didn't last long because it always led to acknowledging I was alone again and that I might never find the "right" person...because ultimately, there was something wrong with me.

Wow. Awesome depressive thought, Maura. You should write greeting cards.

When Sydney's birthday rolled around four weeks post-breakup – not that I cared enough to keep track – I was happy there was finally a distraction from the thought of my impending spinsterhood, at least for one night. Sydney wasn't usually one to have large-scale celebrations, but because of her repeated statements that twenty-six wasn't a big deal, Julie had responded by making it a big deal. She planned for a bunch of us to meet up at R Place. It was a three-story dance club and, of course, outlandishly gay. It was an obnoxious atmosphere that Sydney had only tolerated once on her twenty-one run five years earlier, and neither of us had been there since.

Even though I wasn't looking to meet anybody, especially at a gay bar, I still put extra effort into my hair and makeup. It was just part of the breakup process, attempting to regain some of my self-esteem through vanity. Yet another vice I'm sure Ethan would have been appalled to know I possess. I hated that I thought about him more now that we weren't together than I ever had when we were dating.

That's over. Do not to think about him for the rest of the night.

Julie texted as I approached the club, saying that I didn't have to wait in line outside and could just give the bouncer Sydney's name to be let in. Good news, considering the line outside was already over twenty people deep. Effortlessly, I was let past the rope to enter inside. I scanned the room, glad when my eyes landed on Julie, standing by a table in the back corner. I quickly made my way over to her.

"Maura!" she greeted, giving me a hug. "You got my text about the door, right?"

I nodded, happy that the music wasn't too loud yet, giving me a chance to ease back into the club atmosphere I'd been away from for so long.

"You look cute tonight," she complimented my black lace tank top and royal blue camisole.

"So do you. I guess being engaged agrees with you," I smiled. "Is Syd drunk yet?"

"Please," she rolled her eyes. "It's a miracle I even got her here tonight. She kept complaining that she was too old to be going out to a club."

"I'll get her loosened up for you."

"That's exactly why you're here," she smiled back. Before heading over to the other side of the booth where Sydney was, I went to the bar to get her a drink. I ordered two Hurricanes, specifically requesting a light up glass with a pink umbrella. Julie exchanged an amused look with me when she saw what I was carrying.

"Happy birthday, Syd!" I exclaimed, handing her the obnoxiously girly drink, not caring that I had interrupted her conversation with someone I had yet to meet. She looked at the flashing rainbow glass and then up at me. A sigh escaped her mouth as she reluctantly took it from my hands.

I grinned and held up my glass. "Cheers!"

"Glad you could make it, Maura," Sydney clinked glasses with me. She dramatically grimaced after taking a drink. "At least one of us is embracing this absurdity."

"You know, it was incredibly thoughtful of Julie to plan this for you."

"Maura, I proposed. You don't have to keep talking her up to me."

I sighed.

"Yes, I know, she's priceless. I'm very lucky," Sydney recited accommodatingly.

"See, was that so hard to say?"

"Not half as hard as drinking this," she coughed while taking her second drink.

"Oh, honestly, Syd, stop being such a little bitch and just drink it," I said.

Her mouth dropped open, followed by a proud smile. She slapped me on the back.

"Oh! Mouthy Maurie showed up tonight! I haven't seen her in a long time."

I threw her a pointed look.

"Now this...this is going to be a good night," she proclaimed. "Seriously. Best. Present. Ever."

I rolled my eyes and took another drink.

It's a little-known fact about me that I become extremely smart-mouthed and blunt when drunk. Sydney loved it but she hadn't seen it happen since we were in grad school. And since I had driven myself, I hadn't planned on indulging enough to let "Mouthy Maurie," as Syd liked to call her, show up tonight. Sydney continued to look at me expectantly, knowing she could peer pressure me into just about anything.

"It's not happening," I declared.

"Sounds like a challenge."

"Maybe if you stop nursing your drink, I'll take you seriously enough to consider it," I threw back at her.

Sydney smiled. "Sounds good...Mouthy Maurie," she teased before downing the drink she hated.

Before I knew it, I was on my third Jameson and Ginger. Sydney had been fair and was matching me drink for drink. But as anticipated, she was not showing the effects of any of it. I, however, had announced that she needed to wear a white tuxedo for her wedding because it was "classy as shit, just like Boyz II Men." Luckily, I hadn't serenaded anyone with End of the Road...yet.

I was at the bar ordering Sydney another drink when I turned around to see Thomas walking up to her and Julie. I hadn't seen or heard from him since the gala. I assumed he was too busy having gratuitous, obnoxious, premarital sex with Ashland to have even thought of contacting me. Not that I was bitter. I mean, I'm sure Ashland's egocentric tales of being more enlightened than everyone around her, along with her skinny ass, were far more entertaining than any sort of banter I could offer.

He was wearing khaki cargo shorts and a blue T-shirt. His skin looked even more tan against the light shade of blue. Even though he was dressed more casually than the last time I'd seen him at the gala, he looked just as handsome.

Stop staring. You're on the rebound. That is the only reason you think he's attractive right now.

Yeah, but you thought he was attractive at the gala, and you weren't on the rebound then, I argued against myself.

To prove to myself that I didn't care, I grabbed Sydney's drink and made my way back to the table, cutting in front of Thomas. My back brushed up against his chest.

"Here you go," I said.

"Thanks, buddy," Sydney grinned. "Look who made it out tonight," she gestured to Thomas.

"Hey Maura."

"Hey," I said as nonchalantly as I could, waiting for Ashland to appear out of nowhere, looking, as always, too goddamn gorgeous to be fair.

"Didn't think you'd be at a gay bar," I declared flatly, trying to sound unimpressed. Sydney and Julie snickered, indicating that I clearly was not playing it as cool as I'd wanted to.

"You know, it's good to step outside of your comfort zone every once in a while," he said smoothly. "Plus, I really wanted to dance to YMCA tonight."

I stared at him, unable to think of a retort.

"I was going to go get a drink; do you want anything?" he offered.

"She'll have another Jameson and Ginger," Sydney announced before I could turn him down. I scowled at her once he left.

"What? I thought straight girls loved it when guys bought them drinks," she feigned innocence.

I crossed my arms. Sydney patted the seat next to her, instructing me to sit down. I took the invitation, staring at Thomas as he stood at the bar, waiting to order.

"Do you think any guys are going to hit on him?" I asked loudly, not knowing why I cared to ask.

"Nah," Sydney replied. "I mean, the cargo shorts and flip flops alone are a definite giveaway that he's straight. He would have been in more trouble if he wore the coveralls."

"I know, right?" I exclaimed reflexively, turning to Sydney.

She raised an eyebrow.

"Oh, shut up," was all I could muster.

Thomas returned with my drink and a beer for himself. He sat down next to me.

"So, where's Ashland?" Might as well find out where my looming buzzkill was located.

"I don't know," he shrugged. "I'm not seeing her anymore."

I stared at him. I wanted more of an explanation but was too prideful to ask. Just as I had been too prideful to text him over the past month.

"She kind of..." he paused, apparently trying to pick the right words, "...hated Catholics, and that ended up being a problem for me. You know, since I'm pretty fond of the Catholics that I know."

He smiled and took a drink. I tried to think of something clever to say.

"Well, I never liked her. I mean, what kind of a name is Ashland anyway? It's not a name. It's a mountain, for God's sake, and it's not even a very important one, like Olympus or Rainier."

The words sounded eloquent before I said them. Once they were out of my mouth it was obvious that they were not. Thankfully, Thomas grinned but held back from laughing at me.

"So, where's Ethan? Did he already head upstairs to get a good spot for the cabaret show?"

"Please," I dismissed. "We broke up like a month ago."

"Well, I'm sorry to hear that," he sounded genuine, but not surprised.

"Bullshit," I blurted. "You never liked him."

Thomas laughed.

"No, you're right, I didn't." He took a drink from his beer and then turned to me. "He was far too boring to really appreciate you anyway. Fuck Edwin."

"No, no, Ethan," I corrected, touching his arm.

"Oh, my bad. I seem to have forgotten already." He winked at me. A laugh escaped my mouth, more amused than I normally would've been. He knew I was drunk and there was no way for me to attempt to hide it anymore.

"You know," I sighed, "you're totally right. He was absolutely boring. Especially when it came to making out," I shared without thinking. "I mean, sometimes you just really want someone to play with your breasts," I remarked.

He coughed on his drink.

"Uh-huh, yeah, I totally get that." He tried to keep a straight face but started grinning.

"Whatever," I tried to hide my embarrassment. I took another drink. If I could maintain my buzz, then maybe I would be able to get through the night without overanalyzing everything and just enjoy Thomas' company instead.

THOMAS

I stood at the bar, waiting for the bartender so I could close out my tab. Sydney approached me.

"Thanks again for coming out, man." She patted me on the back as she placed her empty glass on the bar. She had had quite a few drinks, and it was impressive how unaffected she was.

"No problem – happy birthday. Thanks for inviting me."

I was glad to have an excuse to see Maura again. I don't know why I hadn't just called her over the past month...well, that's a lie. Father Sean's relentlessly suggesting that I was interested in her - or should be interested in her - had wormed its way into my consciousness, so naturally, I responded by making a point not to see her or talk to her. Unfortunately, my tried and true method of ignoring things I didn't want to deal with, such as caring about someone, did not work. My brilliant plan had only made me miss her.

"Did you want anything else before I close out my tab?" I asked Sydney.

"Nah, man, I'm good," she turned me down. I attempted to get the bartender's attention and failed for the third time. "You probably should've dressed a little nicer. Maybe worn a V-neck," Sydney informed.

"Mistakes of a first timer, I guess."

"It's good they're taking their time anyway. It'll give you an opportunity to watch this." She turned me around to face the dance floor.

Maura was surrounded by people, not all of them from Sydney's party. She was dancing – more provocatively than I would've ever expected – but also shockingly well and on beat. Sydney laughed at my expression.

"Wasn't expecting to see that tonight," I said. "Where did she learn to do that?"

"Her roommate freshman year. Maura used to go babysit her at all the frat parties. You know, make sure no one took advantage of her and she got home safe. The roommate insisted that if Maura went, she had to at least blend in, so she taught her how to dance," Sydney said, amused. "But I haven't seen the fly girl moves in at least three years."

Maura dropped down and pulled her body back up slowly with her ass in the air. Sydney cat called at her and turned back to me. "I fucking love it," she laughed. Dumbfounded, I continued to stare at Maura. "So, clearly she can't drive," Sydney said. "Would you be able to get our tiny dancer over there home?"

"Sure, I took the light rail here anyway." I finally got a bartender's attention. "I'm closing out," I yelled over the music. He nodded and went to cash me out.

"Syd! Syd!" I heard Maura call out. I turned around. "Syd! Her name's Molly! I'm dancing with Molly! Just like Miley Cyrus!" Maura exclaimed excitedly, pointing at an unfamiliar woman dancing next to her. The woman started moving in closer and was clearly eyeing her. Maura continued to dance, clueless to the advances being made.

"Okay," Sydney said, as we both instinctively moved away from the bar towards the dance floor to run interference.

"I got it," I assured. I grabbed Maura's hand and pulled her away from the floor. She looked at me, confused, but followed without a protest.

"Those are some moves you got there, McCormick." I moved her against the wall.

"You want me to teach you? It's super easy," she yelled. "You just gotta loosen up your hips," she instructed, trying to wiggle my hips for me.

At least she was a happy drunk.

I moved my hands over hers and looked her in the eye. "You know, I think I'm going to have to take a rain check. I don't think you're ready for this jelly."

"Oh puh-lease," she scoffed. "You hardly have any ass at all." She reached behind me, squeezing one side of my butt. I was caught off guard and jumped back.

"Whoa, okay," I exclaimed with a laugh, not really sure if she was flirting or just being herself with alcohol. "You're going to have to at least buy me dinner first," I joked.

"Fine, how's next Tuesday?"

And now I couldn't tell if she was serious or messing with me.

"That is, unless, you're planning on sleeping with another one of our interns by then."

It took me a second, but I realized she was referring to Ashland.

"I never slept with Ashland," I shared, talking loudly in her ear.

She pulled away and gave me a doubtful smirk.

"I didn't," I reiterated. "She just wasn't worth it."

Her expression registered belief.

"You know, kind of like guys who buy you skis for your birthday, even though you hate skiing." I held her stare for a moment, and thought for a second about kissing her, but hesitated, thinking Sydney might kick my ass if I did.

"Sydney asked me to drive you home," I said instead. "Can I get your keys?" She handed them over without needing any convincing.

Once she'd said goodbye to Sydney – which took a while; there was a lot of hugging and "I love you so much, Syd!" – it was a little frustrating trying to get Maura to remember where her car was. We walked around for at least twenty minutes before she was able to direct me to the street where she was parked; she kept getting distracted by pointing out different restaurants she had been meaning to try. The wandering had helped her sober up, so that was good – and it prolonged my time with her, so that was nice too.

Since she had already proven herself to be horrible navigator, I was thankful I didn't have to rely on her to direct me back to her apartment. Maura was happy not to have to play co-pilot since it allowed her to focus on singing every single song that came on the radio, because each one was her favorite of all time – obviously. I concluded she was a better dancer than singer.

Once we got back to her apartment, I thought that she would head upstairs and the night would be over. But after I handed her keys back to her, she linked arms with me and led me out of the garage and onto the street.

"You know, Thomas, I really love the birthday present you gave me," she said emphatically.

"Oh? Thank you, I'm glad you do."

"I think it's, like, my favorite present ever, in the history of birthdays."

"Wow, in the history of birthdays?" I said with feigned awe. "Well, I don't know if it's that good." We stopped walking.

"No, no, it is," she argued. "Sitting by that statue is one of my favorite places, and I never even told you, but you just knew it was special."

"I did," I affirmed quietly.

"And you said you didn't even paint anymore. But then you painted that...for me."

"I know, I was there," I laughed, hoping she wasn't going to ask me why I had changed my mind.

"Why?"

No such luck.

I looked down at my feet, trying to think of an answer that would make sense but not lead her to think she meant as much to me as she actually did.

"I guess when I said I didn't paint anymore, what I really meant was that I didn't feel like painting anymore...but when I saw you sitting there on Easter, for the first time in a long time, I felt the same as when I first started painting...it's hard to describe, other than this intense need to put what I see onto a canvas...so I did. I'm not sure when I'm going to get that feeling again, but I guess it's not completely gone like I thought it was."

I held back from thanking her. Maybe someday I would tell her how much it meant to get that feeling back, but not tonight.

She nodded but didn't say anything. Once again, I expected her to leave and conclude the night, but I didn't want to be the first to say goodnight. Maura paused for a moment.

"Guess what?" she gave me a mischievous grin. "Race you to Teddy's!" She took off down the sidewalk.

Worried that she would run into traffic, I chased after her. I caught up to her as she turned the corner, and we both reached the door at the same time.

"Okay, okay, okay," she laughed, trying to catch her breath and gain composure. "Thomas, you're gonna have to lock it in before we go in there," she instructed seriously.

"Oh, really? I'm the one that needs to lock it in?" I laughed.

She nodded. "On weekends this place is crawling with hipsters. It's no place for obnoxious drunks."

"Well in that case, maybe we should get you home."

"No, I need to buy you a drink for your birthday," she explained.

"Maura, my birthday's in December."

"Exactly. And I missed it. I feel really terrible about it, so I have to make it up to you."

"Maura, last December, I was still living in New York. We didn't know each other." Trying to be the voice of reason was pointless, but I still gave it a shot.

"Unacceptable. It was rude of me to forget," she declared, opening the door.

She was right about the clientele at Teddy's on a Saturday night. The place was loaded with dark framed glasses and flannel. The low drone of voices and quiet filled the air. It was the complete opposite of the bar we had come from. Maura sat down directly at the bar and waited, successfully holding her composure. I joined her.

"What can I get you?" The bartender approached.

"He'll have a Three Wise Men," she ordered for me. "And I'll have a–"

"Water," I interrupted to complete her order, not wanting her to undo the progress she had made sobering up. She gave me a pointed look then turned back to the bartender.

"And a Stella," she finished. The bartender nodded and walked away.

"Three Wise Men?"

"Get it? 'Cause your birthday's in December. Like Jesus," she added just in case I didn't fully put it together. The bartender returned with the cocktail of hard liquor and pints of both water and beer. I pulled the beer towards myself while Maura was distracted by paying the tab.

She frowned when she saw only water in front of her.

"Drink your water first, then we'll talk."

She didn't argue and took a drink. I stared reluctantly at the cocktail of straight tequila, whiskey, and scotch. The easiest thing to do would be to shoot it and get it over with. Had anybody ever honestly ordered this drink with the intention of savoring it? I concealed the cough I wanted to let out after downing it. Maura looked at me wide eyed, expecting a response.

"How about next time, you just get me eggnog?"

She opened her mouth, ready to get the bartender's attention. I forced her hand down. "Maura, they don't have eggnog."

"Well, they should."

I laughed at how serious she sounded.

"Can I get you something else?" she asked.

"I'm thinking I really want this beer here." I moved the pint over to myself, preventing her from drinking more alcohol or buying me more god-awful shots.

"Fair enough." She took another drink of her water, continuing to sober.

"I don't think this crowd could handle your drunken dance moves anyway." I signaled at the bartender to bring her more water when she finished her glass.

"I'm really glad you moved back," she said, ignoring my teasing. I stared at her, thinking the same thing.

When I didn't say anything, a look of panic crossed her face. "Oh, shit, I'm sorry. I didn't mean I'm glad your dad died."

"No, no, Maura, I knew what you meant," I assured her. "I'm glad I moved back, too." There was a lull while she focused on drinking her second glass of water. "Care to shoot some pool?" I attempted to lighten the mood again.

She shook her head. "I don't like pool. I'm not very good at it."

"Maybe you'd like it more if I gave you condescending male advice while we played?"

"Sure thing, Sean," she said dryly.

"What games are you good at then?"

"Hmm," she paused to think, ordering a third glass of water. While she was busy becoming more of sound mind, I was starting the feel the effects of my drinks. "Well, I don't mean to brag, but I was the tetherball champion in fifth grade."

"Oh, wow, tetherball champion," I marveled sarcastically. "I don't think I've ever met one of those before. You must have lightning fast reflexes."

"Mmmhmm," she agreed. "And I'm strategic. That is also why I am the best at Uno."

"Uno?" I scoffed, thinking the two games had nothing in common.

"What?"

"I hate to break it to you, but I don't think there's much strategy or reflexes involved in the game Uno."

"Yeah-huh," she argued, which only made me smile more. "It's totally a game of strategy and you have to have quick reflexes to say, 'Uno!' when you have one card left."

"Maura, it's the luck of the cards you're dealt."

"You wanna bet? I will kick your ass at Uno anytime," she challenged.

"Well, unfortunately, I don't think a fine establishment like this keeps a deck of Uno cards handy."

She downed the rest of her water and stood up.

"I have a deck at home. Come on, let's go. You and me, O'Hollaren." She poked my shoulder.

"Are you serious?"

"You got anything better to do?" She had her hands on her hips. Her effort to be menacing was adorable. "Now stop babysitting that beer and let's go."

I followed her instructions, taking a couple large drinks before following her out the door.

She continued her humorous attempt to intimidate me throughout the walk back to her apartment. After each threat and declaration, I would challenge her, just to keep her going. What was most amusing was that she was no longer drunk, and this was completely sober Maura behavior – harassing someone you were about to play a child's card game against. Given my tipsy state, I would probably just let her win, but she didn't need to know that. This was by far the most innocent of circumstances that had ever led me back to a woman's apartment after being at a bar.

"Hang on, I'm going to go change," she said when I closed the door behind us. I turned to see her walking into her bedroom and lifting up her shirt, revealing the back of a black bra.

The fact that she even owned black underwear was probably the most intriguing thing I had discovered in my time knowing her. I waited a few moments, pleased with myself when I saw the painting I had given her hanging up on the wall by her table. She really did like it. I went into her room and sat down on the bed.

"I know they're here somewhere," she said as she searched through her closet. She was wearing a maroon t-shirt that appeared to be from some 5k that she had run, undoubtedly for charity. What caught my attention more was the short pajama bottoms she had put on. When Maura bent over to look into the closet, the descriptor 'booty shorts' came to mind. After a few more moments of searching, she stood up, completely oblivious that I had been eyeing her.

"Well, I guess I don't have my Uno cards here." She turned to me. "Maybe they're at work."

"That's a shame. I guess we're just going to have to end the night without knowing who the ultimate Uno champ is," I feigned disappointment and laid down on the bed.

"What're you doing?"

"Taking a quick rest before going home. I can't leave now, not after the three shots and beer you insisted I drink." Truthfully, I could've endured the twenty-minute walk home. I just didn't want to leave, especially now that she was wearing those shorts.

"Well, you're on my side." She nudged me on the shoulder.

"But, I'm the guest. The guest always gets to pick which side of the bed they want to sleep on," I said innocently, wanting to aggravate her.

"No, that's not how it goes."

"Um, I'm pretty sure it is. If you want me to move, you're going to have to make me. It shouldn't be too hard. I mean, with all those muscles you have from playing tetherball and Uno."

She knelt on the bed and tried, very unsuccessfully, to move me. Her lack of upper body strength was pathetic. What I did not expect was for her to tickle me. I jerked back and grabbed her arms before rolling her over onto the other side of the bed. I continued to hold her hands away from me, both of us laughing.

She looked up at me, smiling, and I finally got the courage to do it; I leaned in and kissed her. It was the only time I had ever initiated a first kiss. Since I was twelve, I'd always waited for the girl to take charge on any initial encounter. I prolonged the kiss, partly because her lips felt so good, but also because I feared what Maura would say when I broke away. After a few wonderful seconds, she finally pulled away.

"Well, I guess you can stay on that side of the bed for tonight, if you really want to."

I immediately kissed her again, this time more assertively, introducing my tongue. She reciprocated. I had not expected Maura to be that good of a kisser. Normally I would have moved on to other things at this point, but I didn't. I just kept kissing her for what felt like a perfect eternity.

She had turned onto her back and I fought every instinct I had to get on top of her. I didn't want to seem too presumptuous. I was already pressing my luck by making out with her on a bed. However, being one to push limits, I ran my hand up her leg. God, her skin was soft. The loose fabric at the leg of her shorts had fallen up, leaving the top of her thigh exposed. I heard her breath catch as I moved my hand up her thigh to squeeze the top of it.

I kept kissing her, not sure where the whole interaction was going, yet completely content in the moment. The side of my shirt started to rise; Maura was lifting it up while we continued to kiss. I pulled away briefly, allowing her to finish removing it. Okay, so that was surprising. I returned to her mouth, happily feeling the sensation of her hands moving around my naked torso. Our breath had quickened at that point. I was thoroughly enjoying the rise of her chest against mine, even if it was still covered by that stupid shirt – I didn't think she would be as willing to lose it as I was with mine.

Maura's hands moved down to the waist of my shorts. She started fumbling with the button. I pulled back and looked at her questioningly.

"Aren't you kind of hot in these?" She held my stare as she pulled them down. There seemed to be a mutual agreement that undressing me was fair game. I maneuvered the shorts off and hovered above her, just in my boxers. As I rested down and she wrapped her legs around me, instinctively, we both started moving our hips up and down.

Okay, I knew where this was heading, or at least where it looked like it was heading. I pulled away. I couldn't help but appreciate how breathtaking she looked lying there beneath me; her golden hair laying on the pillow, surrounding her beautiful face. She probably hadn't been this far before, or if she had, it wasn't with someone like me.

"Maura, what are we doing?" I had to clarify what was going on.

"Having fun." She propped herself up on her elbows, closer to my face. "At least, I think you're having fun," she whispered, raising an eyebrow suggestively. "Because I can feel your erection," she sing-songed playfully, falling back and giggling. With anybody else, this would have killed the mood, but not with her. I bent down and kissed the side of her neck, running my hand through her hair. She responded by squeezing my body with her thighs.

The voice inside my head told me that regardless of Maura's reaction, I had to stop. It was difficult to give this voice credence because Maura was giving me every sign that every woman before her had given me to keep going. I decided to ignore that voice for the time being and went back to Maura's lips while my hand found its way back to the outside of her thigh.

Maura propped herself up on her elbows, remaining attached to my lips. I pulled away, expecting her to announce that the whole encounter had to stop. She surprised me again, this time by pulling off her shirt. There was that black bra again. I felt myself grow harder as I took in her cleavage.

I looked back into her eyes. She looked pretty damn sure of herself. Her hands moved up and down my chest, the touch firmer than I expected from someone so inexperienced. I tilted my head down to take a breath and attempted to regain my composure.

"How far do you want this to go, McCormick?" I finally asked when I looked back up. She closed her eyes and pulled me back to her lips.

"I'll tell you when you need to stop," she whispered as we started kissing again.

There I had it; Maura had given me permission to keep going, barring some dramatic realization that she shouldn't be fooling around with me. I ordered myself not to go past third base, regardless of how much of her body she allowed me to see that night. I didn't want to press further for more information from her, mostly because the more we talked, the more likely she would be to put an end to what we were doing.

While I tried to contemplate what Maura would consider appropriate third base physicality, she continued kissing me, now taking her turn to move to my neck and ear. I couldn't remember the last time I had spent this long on foreplay and actually enjoyed it. I recalled the comment she made earlier, lamenting that Ethan never played with her breasts and took the liberty to start gently squeezing and kissing the outline of them.

As I kissed her breasts over the lacy fabric, I wondered again whether she had ever been this far with another person. I had mixed emotions when it crossed my mind that I might be the first man to get this far. Admittedly, it inflated my ego to assume I was the only one. At the same time, there was a sense that I probably wasn't a good enough person to be allowed to do such things with her. She was arching her back as I remained connected to her chest, and she finally let out her first moan of the evening, albeit a quiet one. I fought back the urge to remove the garment altogether. When the thought became too tempting, I moved down to her stomach.

Her eyes were closed in an expression of enjoyment. I took my time kissing her stomach, and eventually gently licking around her belly button. Maura's breath caught and she moved her torso up and down, pressing her pelvis to me, communicating she wanted more. Which I was gladly ready to give.

In the past, I had wanted the woman to climax solely so that I could feel my own sense of accomplishment. But in that moment, I wanted to make Maura feel something amazing. I had never been so consumed with someone else achieving orgasm while I received nothing on the other end of it.

Did oral sex constitute further than third base? I moved my mouth down to the waistband of her shorts to test the waters. She ran her fingers through my hair, but I felt her pull her legs together under my chest. Okay, too far. I pulled back up, still determined to hear that beautiful moan again. I rested myself on my side next to her, my hand cupping her breast as I kissed the side of her neck and collarbone.

I gave her a moment to tell me to stop, but held back from asking her. When she said nothing, my hand gradually made its way down, caressing the softness of her abdomen and between her legs, over her shorts. I pushed gently and heard that wonderful quiet moan again, followed by Maura catching her breath. I teased her and moved my fingers to her inner thighs tracing them up and down, enjoying the sound of her moan while Maura ran her fingers through my hair.

I bent down and kissed her lips, feeling her press more deeply and passionately than before; I was doing something right. I moved my hand back between her thighs and began to rub softly. The moan came louder now, but I didn't think she was going to come with my hand on the outside of her clothing.

Hoping it was permissible to eliminate just one barrier, I boldly reached my hand down the front of her shorts, half expecting her to pull my hand away. I pressed in the same circular motion, pleased that her breath had quickened and the moans came more frequently. I kept up the motion, moving my hand faster and more insistently against her, feeling Maura raise her hips up and down, gripping the side of my arm.

She kept her eyes closed. I was transfixed watching her. She alternated from biting her lip to moaning with open pleasure, and finally ending with a deep sigh as she arched her back. She collapsed, breathless. A small smile appeared on her face and she opened her eyes at me dreamily. I realized for the first time how sweaty we both were given the summer heat and the lack of air conditioning in her apartment. We remained on top of the covers as both of our heart rates slowed down.

"Well," she sighed, sounding half asleep, "now I know how Kyle Seager feels." I couldn't help but let out a laugh at her obscure reference to the Mariners' third baseman.

"You know how ridiculous you are, McCormick?" I said, resting down on my side, alleviating my shoulder that had begun to cramp. She rolled over and I held her in my arms.

"You know you love it," she said simply, keeping her eyes closed. I didn't say anything, running my hands gently through her hair. It only took a few moments before she was sound asleep. I continued to enjoy feeling the softness of her skin. She was right; I did love her randomness and sense of humor, but more importantly, I loved her. I drifted off to sleep as I held her my arms, feeling a happiness I had never felt before.

MAURA

It was the best sleep I had had in months. It was the type of sleep you slip into seamlessly, only to wake up hours later feeling like you had just closed your eyes. As I started to stir, I felt the throw blanket from my couch on top of my mostly naked body. It registered that I was being held by somebody. Suddenly, the memories of the previous night with Thomas flooded my mind.

Fuck. Fuck. Fuuuuuuuuuck. My eyes flashed open. Maybe I had dreamed the whole thing? Nope. Thomas' arm was wrapped around me. Every muscle in my body tensed. I stared forward like a deer caught in headlights. I worried that it would wake him up if I went back to breathing normally or moved at all. I had no idea what I would say to him. Or worse, what he would say to me.

What the hell had I been thinking? Could I blame it on being drunk? No. I remembered the entire night...the entire encounter... and knew I'd been completely in control of my decisions, particularly at the end of the night. The alcohol had just served as a veil, an excuse for being uninhibited. Damn it. Apparently, I thought the logical decision after breaking up with Ethan was to become a slut.

Yes, of course, I knew most people, in this day and age, would not consider what I had done very high up there on the slut-scale... but for me, making out with a guy who was not my boyfriend, while we were both in our underwear, to the point of orgasm, was pretty damn slutty. Especially when I had chosen to do it with a guy who considered that type of interaction with a female to be part of the status quo. Shit.

I felt him stir and he moved his arm slightly. I hoped that he would remain asleep and I could somehow get out of the bed without him noticing. I inched my body towards the edge of the bed. His hand moved down to my waist and I froze again.

"Morning," he said sleepily. I contemplated pretending like I was still asleep but decided it would only make the situation more awkward.

"Morning," I returned quietly. His lips touched my shoulder and then started to trail up my neck. Before I let it completely register just how good it felt, I sat up, holding the blanket to myself, still keeping my back to him. I quickly scanned the floor for my shirt, sadly realizing it was on the on the other side of the bed. He gently touched my back.

"You started to shiver in the middle of the night, so I grabbed that blanket off your couch. I didn't want to wake you up to get under the covers."

I didn't know if he expected me to thank him. I didn't. I just nodded.

I got up, still holding the blanket over my chest, not caring that I pulled it away from him. Even though I still had my bra on, I didn't want to walk around in front of him without a shirt on. Yes, this seemed inconsistent, given what I had done with him the night before. I still couldn't look at him. I quickly found my shirt and put it on, then went to look at my phone to see what time it was. Anything to keep from looking at him, even though I was acutely aware that he was staring at me.

"So, do you have any plans today besides Mass?" Thomas was now sitting up with his arms propped on his bent knees. Of course he could sound so casual in this circumstance, given the number of times he had undoubtedly been in it before.

I ignored his question and kept my eyes locked on my phone, trying to decide whether I should go to Mass at all, feeling too guilty to even set foot in a church.

"Because I was thinking we could go get some pancakes," he suggested.

"Um, I'm not really hungry." The guilt had firmly settled itself into my stomach by that point.

"Well," he said as he grabbed the phone from my hands to place it back down on the nightstand.

I finally looked at him for the first time that morning.

"Maybe I could help you...." he put both of his hands on my hips and turned me back down onto the bed "...work up an appetite."

He kissed my neck as his hand went up the side of my thigh, bringing back the memory of how everything had started the night before. I quickly broke away and sat up, brushing his hand away. He sat up next to me and looked at me with confusion.

"Is my morning breath that bad?" he joked.

I didn't answer.

"Something wrong?"

I remained silent.

"Okay." He rubbed the back of his neck.

Not wanting to risk him kissing me again, I stood up.

"So, obviously last night..." I attempted to explain, but faltered as he stared at me. "Look, Thomas, I don't do what I did last night," I fumbled.

"But you did," he countered. "With me," he added proudly.

I let out a sigh.

"I didn't mean to," I told him.

He let out a laugh. It was warranted. I knew I had no excuse for what had happened, but that didn't mean I wasn't going to try and find one.

"It's this whole breakup with Ethan," I blurted. "It's just been really upsetting and I guess I was just lonely, and–"

"Horny," he filled in.

I pursed my lips. I hated how relaxed he looked while I stood there completely flustered, still confused by my uncharacteristic actions.

"We obviously drank too much last night," I explained. "And we made a mistake."

I finally looked into his eyes to see if he was accepting any of my explanation. He stood up in front of me. Before I could back away, his hand was on my hip again. I didn't attempt to move, knowing I liked being close to him more than I should have.

"See, I've made a lot of mistakes," he said calmly, "but I'm pretty confident in saying that last night wasn't one of them."

Before I knew it, his mouth was on mine, and we were kissing again. Damn it. Why did he have to be such a good kisser? It had become extremely evident last night when Thomas first kissed me that the whole time I'd been with Ethan, I had been trying to talk myself into thinking I enjoyed kissing him more than I actually did. As I stood there letting Thomas kiss me, it was as if I hadn't been kissed properly in such a long time that I physically would not allow myself to break away, unsure of the next time it would happen.

The kiss was becoming somewhat uncomfortable, given our height difference, and I started to wish he would pull me down on the bed again. When he didn't, I contemplated pulling him down onto the bed instead. I would be playing with fire if I took that step, likely ending up in the same position I'd been in the night before, if not worse.

But I had already made that mistake once, so was it that big of a deal if I ended up making it again? I mean, I already had to go to confession anyway. Thomas moved his lips down to my neck and I opened my eyes to see my crucifix hanging above my door.

"Okay, no," I announced, pushing away from Thomas and catching my breath. "We can't do this again," I tried to sound determined. To be safe, I moved to the other side of the room.

"Why not? We're pretty good at it."

I desperately wanted him to put clothes on so that I wouldn't have to think about how defined his abs were or what his skin felt like against mine.

"Look, I know you're used to doing this...and more...but I don't do this," I reiterated.

"But you did," he repeated, "with me."

"Yes. And I shouldn't have. I mean – what did you expect? That I would just wake up and want to keep fooling around with you?"

"I don't know, Maura, I hadn't really thought beyond wanting to take you out to breakfast this morning," he said simply.

"Oh, is that how you normally thank your conquests after getting what you want?" For some reason, I thought it was best to project my shame onto him.

"Maura, what are you talking about?" He sounded legitimately confused, but I had convinced myself that his intentions could be nothing but selfish.

"Don't think I don't know that you were plotting this to embarrass me," I accused.

"Plotting what?"

"The whole casual, meaningless sex thing. Oh, it would be so funny to prove that Maura is just as bad as everybody else when it comes to self-control."

"You think last night was meaningless?" he raised his voice.

"What else would it be, Thomas? Like you're even capable of anything else," I said bluntly.

Without saying anything, he put his shorts on and grabbed his shirt.

Had I offended him?

He finished pulling on his shirt and walked past me into the living room. I followed him.

"Well, the least you could do is apologize," I irrationally demanded, thinking that's what most guys I had dated would have done.

"What?" he laughed with disbelief as he turned to me. "Apologize for what? For giving you an orgasm and not getting one in return?"

I crossed my arms, uncomfortable with how blunt he was being. I still looked at him expectantly, trying to maintain some sense of righteousness. His eyes grew wide in response to my look.

"Oh, I see. You think I took advantage of you." He shook his head. "Look Maura, it's fine if the other guys want to be the champions of your purity, but I never claimed that responsibility. And frankly, I think it's bullshit for you, as an adult, to let things get that far, consent multiple times, and still expect someone else to apologize when you're the one who didn't uphold your own ridiculous standards," he critiqued, grabbing his wallet and phone off the kitchen counter. "If you want to be pissed off at someone, look in the mirror."

He moved to the door and slipped his sandals on. "And for the record, nothing about last night was meaningless or casual to me," he said pointedly. "I thought I knew you well enough to expect the same from you."

"Oh, like I'm really supposed to believe that?" I defended. "You're the one who's always insisted that every guy is just looking to get laid and that you have no desire to have a serious relationship with anyone. You win, Thomas, I had a moment of weakness and you got in my pants. There's no need to lie about your intentions and make me think it was more than it was. The least you could do is be honest."

He had his hand on the doorknob, clearly ready to be done with me, but then he looked up at me.

"Fine." He paused. "Honestly, last night I thought I had a shot with you."

"A shot with me? What? Like you want to date me?" I said, my tone making the idea sound absurd. I hadn't been expecting him to say that.

He stared back at me, not saying anything, but confirming the question.

"What? Thomas, that's ridiculous," I responded impulsively. "I don't date guys like you."

"I know," he responded quietly, "I guess in the moment, it just didn't seem so unlikely."

We stood there in silence. I was dumbfounded by his confession. I wanted to justify to him why I would never date him, but I couldn't get past the fact that he had admitted to wanting to be with me. I had always assumed I was the last person on earth that he would even consider wanting a romantic relationship with.

"Okay," he said again, just as quietly. "I guess I'll see you around then."

He turned and let himself out.

* * *

It was surprisingly easy to go to work on Monday and pretend like nothing had happened. I'd been in back-to-back meetings all day and avoided having Sydney ask the inevitable question of how my Saturday night ended. In my fit of neurosis, I had begun to wonder if Sydney had set me up for the whole thing – but I knew I was the only one to blame for my actions.

By Tuesday morning, Sydney was so distracted with getting ready for her upcoming vacation that she seemed to have forgotten all about Saturday. She was more concerned about coordinating the coverage of her cases while she was on vacation than anything else. Normally, having to take on the entire workload of another person on top of my own for two weeks would have overwhelmed me, but now I welcomed being buried in work...anything to keep from thinking about him.

"So, it looks like the annual summary and plan for River is due in two weeks," I mentioned to Sydney as she sat with her back to me.

"Yeah, you don't have to worry about that. I talked to the county worker and there's an extension. I'll take care of it when I get back."

"Oh that's fine, I can do it," I said, adding it to my list. She turned around and inspected my face.

"You already have to complete three of my intakes and go to four court hearings on top of three IEPs while I'm gone."

"I know," I said breezily and went back to my computer screen before she could examine my eyes too much.

"Okay," she granted, "but don't stress about it if it doesn't get done. The meeting isn't scheduled until the eighth anyway." She turned back to her desk.

We went back to working in silence. I was quite pleased with myself for the way I'd held my composure for the past two days. In the past, a similar situation with a guy would have left me a neurotic mess in front of Sydney. Perhaps it was the fact that I didn't really care about Thomas as much as other guys. That was a lie; I just didn't have the decency to admit to anyone that I had done something wrong.

A few minutes later Sydney got up and grabbed a notepad and pen. She looked over at me. I stared back blankly.

"Are you coming to the meeting?" she asked.

I raised an eyebrow and pulled up my calendar.

"With Sean. It was scheduled like a month ago," she filled in. The blood rushed to my cheeks.

"Oh yeah, of course," I tried to recover, grabbing for various items at my desk, feigning preparedness. Clumsily, I stood up.

"Really? He still has that effect on you?"

I gave her a pointed look but didn't bother to say anything. I followed her to the conference room.

Anxious thoughts flooded my head. Thomas was going to be brought up. I had been in denial about the professional consequences of what I had done Saturday night until that point. Since the program was on break for the summer, he wasn't technically a current volunteer. I probably couldn't get fired if anyone found out. But after the way I had treated him, it was likely he wouldn't want to volunteer anymore.

Take a deep breath and act natural. Maybe he won't come up at all. I snorted to myself. *Now there's a delusion.*

Of course, telling myself to act natural was one thing, but having my body actually achieve that state was impossible. Within seconds of sitting down I started bobbing my leg nervously while I picked at my fingernails. I looked over to see Sydney staring at me while she sat reclined in her chair, relaxed as always.

"What is up with you?" she laughed.

"Nothing. I'm fine. Too much coffee," I lied.

"You'd think you'd never been around a priest before."

Just then Ann and Sean walked in. He was wearing his blacks.

"No white robes today, Father?" Sydney observed, shaking his hand.

"You know, sometimes it's good to break out of the habit," he joked. It was a bad enough joke that I probably would have said it myself.

I didn't respond.

"Wow, not even a laugh from Maura. I guess it wasn't as clever of a pun as I thought." He took a seat and stared at me for a second.

Damn it, he knows something is wrong.

I sat up straight and willed my leg to hold still. He looked over at Ann.

"Thank you for meeting with me. I don't want to take up too much of your time. I just wanted to let everybody know that our Newman donors were extremely impressed with what was put together with the voc-ed program last spring and they would like to continue their support."

"So, are we thinking about expanding to other skill sets?" Sydney asked.

"Not quite yet," Ann shared. "The board of directors and I think that it would be best to grow the program slowly. We had a great first three months, but let's see how we do with offering the program for a full year before we start offering multiple vocational tracks. Maura, your report from last month was great and I think it not only let us know what really worked, but also where we could improve. Before we launch it again in the fall, do you guys have any specific thoughts, beyond what was in the report?"

There was a silence as I continued to hold my breath, hoping that no one would bring up Thomas. Sean, always one to disappoint me, opened his big mouth.

"Well, I don't know if it's been officially decided or not, but I think it would be really great if Thomas O'Hollaren came back as the instructor. From what I saw, he was fantastic with the teenagers and also very knowledgeable." He looked over at Sydney and me for confirmation.

"Maura, you said that Thomas told you in June that he was plan-ning to come back, right?" Ann brought me into the conversation.

"Uh, yes, he did say that last month," I confirmed slowly, evad-ing eye contact with Sean. "But," I paused, "you know, a lot can change over the summer; I'm not sure if he's still interested."

Sydney raised her brow at me.

"Did he say something to you on Saturday?" she asked in a lower tone, trying to direct the question at just me, which was point-less, seeing as how everyone heard her ask it.

"No, not..." I paused, trying to select my words carefully, "not specifically. I just think, you know, with the break over the summer, it's probably a good idea for Ann to confirm that he's still interested, and if not, it will give us time to find a replacement."

Sydney and Sean stared at me, simultaneously trying to read my face. Luckily, Ann was nodding her head.

"That sounds like a good plan, Maura. I'll follow up with him later and hopefully be able to get a commitment. What other feed-back do you guys have?"

"Well, I thought it was good that Sydney and Maura were present for the meetings on Wednesdays," Sean said. "Especially since a crisis response was needed at least once and Maura was able to de-escalate the situation."

"What were your guys' thoughts on that?" Ann turned it back to Sydney and me.

"I thought it was good," Sydney agreed. "And I think Thomas probably found it helpful."

A silence passed.

"So, I was thinking," I prayed that the idea I was about to present wouldn't sound suspicious, "that it might be a good idea if only one of us supported the program, rather than switching off week to week. You know, for the sake of consistency." I paused. "I just feel like, personally, I wasn't super interested in being out in the garage, and it seemed like more of Sydney's forte."

Sydney was going to kill me later for not warning her about the suggestion beforehand, but since I was making it up on the spot, there really had been no opportunity to prep her. "I would be willing to take on extra responsibilities in other areas to make sure the work is distributed fairly."

"Syd, do you have any thoughts about that?" Ann asked before granting my request. I continued to look straight ahead.

"Uh, no, not at the moment," she said calmly, willing to blindly follow my lead.

"Okay, we will look into that as it gets closer to the fall and see what Maura can take off your plate to even things out."

I felt the tension in my muscles release slightly with Ann's response. Hopefully, removing myself from the program would be enough to keep Thomas involved. I would feel so guilty if my one night of carelessness led to the youth losing a competent instructor who they had actually made a connection with. I stayed quiet for the rest of the meeting. Luckily, it didn't last much longer. We were excused. I mumbled a goodbye to Sean before retreating to my desk.

"You want to explain what's going on?" Sydney asked, closing our office door behind her. I stayed silent, not knowing where to start.

"Unless you just really believe that the lesbian is a better fit for auto shop, which was an easy sell to Ann, so I guess you're not the only one pushing the stereotype around here."

I ignored her sarcasm and blurted my explanation. "I had outercourse with Thomas Saturday night."

"Did you just say 'outercourse'?" she asked, more focused on my terminology than my confession.

"Well, it wasn't sex...but you know, things happened," I struggled to articulate.

"What kind of things?"

"You know, the thing that happens when you do that," I remained vague, still too embarrassed to divulge the details with another person.

"Ejaculation?" she searched, still confused.

"No, not that," I exclaimed. "The other thing."

She continued to look at me, not understanding.

"You know, that, but for a girl."

"Jesus, it's like talking to a fourteen-year-old," Sydney said with frustration. "Do you need to draw a picture?"

"Third base," I managed to spit out. "I, you know..." I dropped my voice low, looking to Sydney to fill in the blank. She continued to look at me blankly. I sighed and whispered, "Completed."

"You mean you came? Jesus, Maura, just say it then." She had little patience. "So, he fingered you," she finally concluded, a little too brashly, and loudly, for my liking. "Or was it just dry humping?"

I scoffed at her casual tone.

"What? That's what people say. No one says 'outercourse.' Wait, oral sex could be considered third base too," she added. "Did–"

"No!" I exclaimed before she could ask the question.

"Okay, okay," she held up her hands, signaling for me to calm down.

There was a pause.

"So, you're worried about the whole volunteer relationship policy," she assumed. "I won't tell anybody. And I seriously don't think Ann is going to care if you guys disclose your relationship before he officially comes back on as a volunteer."

"We're not in a relationship." I was short with her, but I didn't really have a right to be frustrated with her for not understanding, especially when I hadn't given her that much information.

"Then what's the problem?" She stared at me. I started to wonder if I really was making a big deal out of nothing. The guilt in the pit of my stomach told me otherwise.

"He sort of told me he was interested in me and I told him that he wasn't capable of ever having a serious relationship...and that I would never date anyone like him," I finally admitted quietly, staring at my desk.

Saying it aloud made it sound as cold as I had suspected it was.

"Oh," Sydney reflected. "Well, then there's that."

We stood in silence for a moment.

She sighed. "We're going to need a new fucking mechanic, aren't we?"

I didn't look at her, knowing she was just as irritated with me as I was with myself.

"Shit, Maura, what were you thinking?"

"I don't know," I raised my voice. "Obviously I wasn't."

"You couldn't have let him down gently?"

"I was in shock. I didn't think he would ever be interested in me."

"Oh, bullshit," she called me out. "Have you never seen the way he looks at you? The way he would always hang around on Wednesday nights just to say goodbye to you? It doesn't take anyone twenty minutes to lock a garage door. Seriously, the grab ass between you two was audible."

"I never noticed," I partially lied.

She threw me a doubtful look.

"Look, I feel bad enough. I don't know why I let it get that far with him. Apparently, there's something wrong with me and this whole stupid break up with Ethan has left me desperate," I presented the rationalization I had been forcing on myself as an explanation.

"Oh yes, because only the desperate result to sexual behavior," she said sarcastically. "My condolences, Maura, but you appear to have a libido, just like the rest of us mere mortals."

"That is not why it happened," I argued, hating to think the whole thing could be explained by something so primitive.

"Then why did it happen?"

"I don't know, he kissed me, and..." I froze, still not knowing what my intentions had been on Saturday. "I don't know, it just happened."

"So, you're expecting me to believe that you, Maura McCormick, went home with someone with the expectation of having a casual hookup in order to get over Ethan?"

"No...yes." I let out a sigh as she continued to look at me expectantly. "When it was happening I just assumed he wasn't going to take it seriously. I didn't know he was going to wake up and want to date me."

"Maura, you really think that after twenty-six years of being a prude, you're really the type to seek out a hand job for the purposes of rebounding?" she asked with disbelief.

"Just for one night," I clarified. "I know, I'm a horrible person. And now I probably wrecked this whole voc-ed program," I finally verbalized my guilt.

I expected her to agree that I was terrible person, but she didn't.

I looked up at her. "What?"

"I'm calling bullshit on this whole newfound whoredom routine," she said matter-of-factly, returning to her usual state of calmness and sitting down at her desk.

"What?"

"Yeah, I'm not buying it," she affirmed. I took a break from my self-inflicted guilt trip to be utterly confused by her reaction. "Don't get me wrong, I'm still upset that we might have to find a new mechanic, but I don't think it's because you got horny. I think it's because you're self-sabotaging."

"I'm not sabotaging anything. Everybody makes mistakes."

"Hmm, yeah, I don't think you made a mistake and I think you know it wasn't a mistake, regardless of how much you want it to be a mistake," she said. "You're obviously attracted to Thomas and you had it all worked out in your head that he wasn't the right guy for you because he doesn't fit whatever expectation you've built up over all these years. And when you gave into that attraction – which by the way, is completely natural and God-given, so let's get over that shame, but anyway – afterwards I'm willing to bet you were disappointed in the fact that one: you enjoyed it as much as you did, and two: he didn't end up being the dick you thought he'd be, which is what you were really hoping for, because it would have allowed you to get over the attraction in the first place.

"So of course you have to go and convince yourself of all the reasons why you can't date him, the biggest one probably being that he's not like any other guy you've ever been with. Who all, by the way, found something wrong with you, regardless of how perfect you tried to be, so I can't fathom why you'd want to keep jumping down that rabbit hole." She paused. "But just because he's not what you expected, that doesn't make him un-dateable, it just makes you scared." She stopped again. "And hence, the sabotage," she finished her point with a wave of her hand.

"Oh, that's great," I said sarcastically with my arms crossed. "Thanks for your analysis that no one asked for."

"You're welcome," she responded smartly.

I decided in that moment to take my lunch break, off site, away from her.

"You're only mad because you know I'm right."

Pretending to ignore her, I grabbed my keys and moved to the door.

"Maura," she stopped me with a softer tone. I expected her to apologize. "Imagine what it would be like to date somebody who didn't make piety a requirement for loving you. It'd be less stressful and, dare I say, a little bit more in line with what you believe."

I left without saying anything, knowing I had nothing to counter her argument.

THOMAS

"Thomas, my man, what was up with you today?" Father Sean asked light-heartedly as he approached the bench. He was referring to the three absent-minded errors I'd made which ultimately cost us the game. Combined with four strikeouts, it was the worst game of baseball I had ever played. I didn't look at him and shrugged while I finished changing out of my cleats.

"I don't know. Guess it's just not my day."

I tossed my glove into my gym bag along with the cleats. Since leaving Maura's apartment on Sunday, I had been unable to focus on any task I'd attempted. Father Sean let out a laugh of disbelief as he replaced his cleats with tennis shoes.

"BS," he called me out. "You want me to believe you played that crappy just 'cause? Nah, clearly, there's something else on your mind."

I sat in silence, hesitant to confirm his suspicions.

"Care to enlighten me, Thomas?" he said in a priestly tone.

I gave him a scornful look.

"Don't get mad at me because you let whatever's bothering you affect my baseball game. Go on without us," he called to the other players waiting on the field. They started walking out of the park. "You didn't want to get beer with them, did you?" he confirmed after the fact.

"No," I said.

"So, you were saying," he prompted.

"I wasn't saying anything." I stood up.

"You sure? I felt like you were about to tell me everything that was bothering you, so I could forgive you for those six errors you made."

"It was three. And are you going to take any responsibility for missing the cut-off man in the third?" I challenged. "Anyway, this is a beer league; you shouldn't be keeping track of errors."

He continued to sit, waiting patiently.

"Don't you have somewhere to be?" I asked curtly.

"Well, I was going to go get a beer, but I decided to check and see if my friend Thomas was okay because he seemed out of sorts. I know, I'm such an asshole," he responded flatly.

"You are literally the last person in the world I want to talk to about this."

"Those are usually the circumstances when talking to a priest comes in handy. Then again, I could be a little biased."

I stared at him, unamused.

"This wouldn't have anything to do with a little blond spitfire we both happen to know, would it?"

I sighed and retook my seat. "How'd you know?" There was no point in lying once he had guessed it was about her.

"I saw her Tuesday."

"What'd she say?" I had called Maura three times and texted twice since Sunday and received no answer. I wanted whatever information I could get.

"Well, besides not looking at me when the topic of you came up, she somehow got the impression you might not be returning as a volunteer in the fall? Of course, she wouldn't say why. Also, she requested to not be involved with the program anymore."

I stared down at my hands, disappointed his account confirmed that Maura wanted nothing to do with me.

"Now," Father Sean continued, "a protective ex-boyfriend's imagination tends to run a little wild when he's left to his own devices to piece together—"

"I didn't sleep with her," I interrupted before he could finish the implication. I made sure to look him in eye. He paused, evaluating whether he believed me.

"I never said I wasn't going to come back in the fall either. Unless that's what she wants." He sat there silently, waiting for me to reveal more.

"I told you this would be a train wreck. I warned you two months ago when you brought it up. I warned you," I said again.

"So, what happened?"

"I met up with her at Sydney's birthday party last Saturday, and she drank too much so I drove her home. When I dropped her off at her place, she decided she wanted to go out around the corner, so we did, but I didn't let her drink anything else. Eventually she sobered up and I went back to her apartment because she..." I paused, knowing how ridiculous it was going to sound, "...really wanted to beat me at Uno."

"Sounds about right," Father Sean laughed. "It is one of her favorite games."

"Anyway, I kissed her. And she kissed me back. I thought she was going to tell me to stop. I even broke away a couple times to ask what we were doing, how far it was going to go, but she just kept going." I stopped and tried to read the expression on his face. I couldn't decipher anything. He didn't look pissed, like I would have expected him to. "Neither of us got naked or anything. I kept it from going all the way, but..."

"Gratification took place," he filled in, saving me from having to go into too much detail.

"Just on her end," I clarified. "It was weird; I've never been in a situation like that before where it wasn't about what I could get out of it. Honestly, I just wanted to make her happy." I paused. "And then when we woke up in the morning, she told me I took advantage of her and made it very clear she wants nothing to do with me from now on."

His only reaction was a nod. A silence passed.

"So, what are you going to do now?" he asked.

"What?"

"What's your plan? What's your next move?" Father Sean asked expectantly.

"I'm sorry, did you not hear me? She wants nothing to do with me. She told me point blank that she doesn't date guys like me."

"No, she doesn't date guys like you were before. But now you're different."

"Excuse me? How am I different?" I found his optimistic tone naive.

"Well, you're in love with her, aren't you?"

Even though it was true, I was surprised he'd jumped to that conclusion. "You know, I've never really done the whole love thing, so I wouldn't know." I wasn't ready to admit it out loud, especially since it was unlikely that Maura would ever reciprocate the feeling.

"Then what's the big deal? Why get upset if it's nothing?" he challenged with a shrug.

I sighed, not particularly enjoying this newfound intimacy. I would much rather stick to talking baseball with Father Sean than talking about my feelings.

"I don't know. Because I fucked up. I read the signals wrong and now she's done with me."

"So? Just another girl in the books, right?"

"She's not just another girl. She's...you know...she's Maura."

"And..." he led expectantly.

"And I care about her," I confessed, annoyed that he'd gotten it out of me.

"Okay, I guess we can settle for the word 'care' if you're too chicken to say 'love,'" he hassled. "If you care about her, don't you kind of have to go after her?"

"Go after her? What do you think this is? A movie?" I laughed off his suggestion.

"Well, at the very least you have to tell her."

"I did tell her. She pretty much laughed me out of her apartment."

"Really? You told her you loved her? Excuse me, I mean, you told her you *cared* about her?" he corrected himself.

"No... but I told her I was interested in her," I clarified

"Oh, well, in that case, that's even more romantic," he said sarcastically.

"I've tried getting a hold of her multiple times. She won't return my calls or my texts. She's done with me," I reiterated.

"Oh, that's right, you like to take the easy way out."

I frowned at him, irritated.

"Look, let me tell you something about Maura: she's great at handling unexpected situations at work, but she's not so great at handling them in her own life. It probably comes with being

Catholic; you know how we like our structure," he joked. "She's had a picture in her mind of exactly the type of guy she's going to end up with since God knows when, and let's face it: you, my friend, are definitely not it."

"Is this supposed to be a pep talk?"

"What I'm saying is, I know her pretty well and I've seen you guys together; I know there's something there. She probably does too. She just doesn't want to recognize it because, somewhere along the line she got the idea that the only acceptable guy to date was an orthodox one who cares more about going to vespers and praying the rosary than being with her."

"Aren't you supposed to love God more than anybody else?" I asked dryly.

"Exactly," he agreed. "And they're all idiots for not realizing that one afternoon with her would leave them believing in God more than any rosary ever could...but you already knew that." He took a deep breath and then patted me on the back as he stood up. "If you really want to be with her, then you have to take a shot and tell her how you feel. Otherwise you're just a coward coasting through life, right?"

"Oh, thanks for that."

"Flattery does not create an honorable man," he said with conviction, hoisting his gym bag over his shoulder.

"Wow, is that written on the wall in the bathroom of the priory or something?"

"Wouldn't you like to know?" he retorted over his shoulder as he started to walk away.

"Wait," I stopped him. "You're not going to say anything about the premarital foreplay I had with your ex-girlfriend?" I was surprised he hadn't admonished me.

"Oh, we're going to cover that when you come to reconciliation on Saturday," he said with a cocky smile, turning away again.

"And what makes you think I'm going to go to confession when I haven't been in over eighteen years?"

"Because you're going to realize that it's only going to help your chances with Maura," he called over as he got further away. "You need all the grace you can get."

His confident tone annoyed me, but I knew he was right.

"Any other advice you want to offer, oh Celibate One?" I called after him, and he turned back.

"Yeah," he said with a grin. "When she finally lets you take her out on a date, don't take her bowling; she hates it." He pointed at me. "Saturday, three o'clock, Blessed Sacrament. I can fit you in before all the holy rollers show up at four."

"An hour?" I clarified with disbelief.

"You said it's been eighteen years; I imagine there's a lot to cover." He turned around and walked away before I could make an excuse.

I couldn't believe that I had come to a point in my life where I was getting relationship advice from a priest – and actually taking it seriously.

* * *

I couldn't think about anything but Maura for the rest of the week. Had I always thought about her this much? I didn't eat anything substantial all week, and I felt the sting of rejection all over again when I tried to call her and got sent straight to voicemail – twice. By Friday, I determined that being in love was not as great as everyone claimed it was. The solution was to get over her.

After we closed the shop for the night, I continued to work, seeking solace in the fact that two cars had been brought in at the last minute. It was eerily quiet in the shop when I started looking over a Lexus to diagnose it. I was okay with the silence; I hoped it would help me focus on the car. But thoughts of Maura quickly surfaced to the forefront of my mind.

I should never have kissed her. Would it have been better if I had never met her in the first place? I couldn't bring myself to believe that. Even though it sucked now, I cared too much about her to wish she'd never come into my life. I'd never been friends with a woman, but she had become that for me...and of course I had to go and ruin it with sex...well, technically not sex, but that seemed to be a moot point.

My mind flooded with all the mistakes I had made towards women in the past. I tallied up all the reasons why Maura was right to declare that she would never be with a guy like me. I lost track of time and was brought back to reality when I heard the door to the front office open. Michael walked into the shop.

"What's up?" I kept my head under the hood.

"Mom sent me over. She said you weren't answering your phone or the office phone, so she got worried."

"I lost track of time," I said simply, still staring at the engine. He stood next to the car as I continued to work.

"What's it look like?"

"Vacuum leak."

"You find the source yet?"

"I used the analyzer, but it doesn't look like the hoses, so probably the manifold."

"You going to leave anything for me and the guys to work on tomorrow?" he kidded.

I shrugged. "I was thinking I would just come in tomorrow, call the owner and get it taken care of."

He gave me a questioning look.

"I'm sure Colleen would appreciate it," I said.

"That's very kind of you, but she's heading up north with the kids and her mom to visit her sister. I'm not about to volunteer myself to go along."

"Wow, eleven years and still not getting along with the sister-in-law," I reflected dryly. "Well, just take the day off anyway. I won't tell her you didn't come in."

He let out a laugh. "Yeah, right."

"Suit yourself, but I'm still coming in tomorrow."

"Tommy, I'm sure there are several more interesting things you can do with your day off than come here."

I didn't respond as I contemplated turning the car on to see if I could find the exact source of the leak.

"Tommy," he tried to get my attention. "Come on, it's almost nine o'clock on a Friday; shouldn't you be out at a bar trying to get laid?" he half joked.

"Yeah, 'cause that's what everybody expects from me any-way, right? I couldn't possibly be trying to run a successful business."

"Man, I was just kidding. You know I appreciate your work. I just don't think you need to be doing it right now at the expense of our mother's nerves."

I moved past him and turned the car back on.

"You know Dad used to do this too," he called over the horri-ble hissing sound the car made while it idled. "He used to stay here and work four, five hours after closing whenever something was bothering him."

"I know." I got up and walked back over to the engine. "I was usually the reason for it," I recalled curtly.

"So you should know it isn't the best strategy for fixing your problems."

"Keeps the bills paid," I bent over, determined to find the leak before I left for the night. Michael wasn't so committed to my mission, turning off the car without asking permission.

"What the fuck? I almost had it," I lied.

"Frank and I will find it tomorrow."

I opened my mouth to argue.

"Tommy, you can't live with Mom and go a whole week without eating dinner and not freak her out," he said matter-of-factly. "Just tell me what's wrong...or go home and tell her what's wrong."

I irresponsibly tossed my wrench back on the workbench, something our dad would have lit into me for if he were there. But he wasn't. He was dead. That's how this whole mess had started anyway, right?

"Mom's convinced you're planning to move back to New York. She's already blaming herself for it," he told me, trying to guilt me into talking.

"I'm not moving back to New York," I declared. "Anyway, what the fuck would you care? You expect me to buy into the whole concerned big brother act?" I snarled, projecting all my frustration about Maura onto him.

"Look, Tommy, I know we've never been close, but...I don't know...it seems like ever since Dad died and you came back, things have been different. It's like you finally want to be part of the family and aren't doing everything in your power to push us away. I know we're not the greatest of pals, but I like having you around," he paused, his discomfort clear, "and if there's anything I can do to keep you around, then I want to...even if it's just for the sake of not having to talk down our overbearing mother at the same time as trying to manage four boys and a wife who's six months pregnant during one of the hottest summers ever."

I stood with my hands on my hips, still feeling the urge to ignore him and turn the car back on to find the source of that damn leak.

"I mean, I know I'm not a priest like your new friend, Father Sean, but I like to think I might have a little insight when it comes to life."

"Please, he was hardly any help at all," I muttered, reflecting on how simple Father Sean had made everything with Maura seem.

"You talked to him?"

"Sort of. He has this way of forcing matters on people."

"Is this about having to work here? I know you never wanted to be a mechanic and you stepped in when we had nobody else."

"No, that's not it." I grabbed a towel and started wiping the grease off my hands. I threw it down. "That's not it at all. I like working here more than I ever thought I would," I admitted. I finally moved over and closed the hood of the car, accepting that I wasn't going to get to work on it for the rest of the night.

"Then what is it?"

I let a silence pass.

"Woman troubles," I mumbled, feeling stupid. It was embarrassing to fess up to being bothered by something so juvenile.

"A woman?" He sounded surprised.

"Yep," I sighed, picking up the wrench I had discarded.

"What woman?"

I hadn't dated anybody to his knowledge since I returned at the end of January. I neatly placed the wrench back in a nearby cabinet.

"Maura."

"McCormick?" I could understand why he was confused. Sometimes even I still couldn't believe how someone like me had gotten involved with someone like her.

"Yep." I waited to see what else he could possibly offer.

"So, you're dating her?"

"No, she's been pretty clear that that will never happen. Unfortunately, like a jackass, I seem to have fallen in love with her. Hence–"

"Hence searching for vacuum leaks in a gasket manifold at nine o'clock on a Friday," he filled in.

"I mean, I really can't blame her for not being interested. You yourself said it, I should be out trying to get laid right now. That's who I am. It's not like I ever tried to be anything better."

"And what'd the priest say?"

"Oh, he was grossly optimistic. Tried to convince me that all I had to do was tell her how I felt and everything would fall into place. But after considering it for the past twenty-four hours, I don't think I should be taking advice from Maura's ex-boyfriend who's now celibate."

"Wait, the priest is her ex-boyfriend?" Michael became more confused with each piece of the story.

"Exactly. So you can see how I am the farthest thing from what she would ever want."

A silence passed. Michael shook his head and let out a laugh. I guess our moment of brotherly bonding was over.

"What?" I demanded.

"Jesus, you are so much like him," he shook his head. "I can't believe neither of you were able to recognize it before. The stubbornness alone should've tipped both of you off. I guess it makes more sense now why you're Mom's favorite."

"What the hell are you talking about?"

"Dad," he answered. "You're just like him. Except the art stuff. We all know you got that from Mom...but everything else; it's all there," he sighed.

Since my dad was the last person in the world I'd ever thought I had anything in common with, Michael's declaration didn't make sense to me. He saw my furrowed brow and realized that I was missing part of the story.

"When Dad was younger, he was part of this motorcycle gang. Nothing serious, mostly street racing and the occasional fist fight. He barely graduated high school and probably wouldn't have found work if Grandpa hadn't owned the shop. I think he even had to stay in jail overnight a few times for disrupting the peace."

I was shocked. All I had ever been told was that my dad used to have a motorcycle but had sold it to buy my mother's engagement ring.

"But then one day, Grandma forced him to go to a church picnic. And that's where he met Mom."

"Wait, no. I thought Mom and Dad dated in high school," I countered.

"Hardly. They went to the same school, but Mom would have never hung out with such a wild crowd. He started going to church just so she would give him the time of day." Michael grinned. "It all makes sense now why you've been coming to mass with us."

"I was going for Mom," I disputed. "I figured it would make up for all those years I upset her by not going."

"Uh-huh," he feigned agreement with a nod. "And who inspired you to do that?"

I paused, knowing he had a point.

He laughed again. "Come on, let's go get a drink, Romeo." He motioned his head towards the door. "I can tell you everything Dad taught me about pursuing women who are too good for you. The first thing being that they're really the only ones worth pursuing in the first place."

MAURA

After struggling all week with deciding whether I should go to confession or not, I willed myself to drive to Blessed Sacrament late Saturday afternoon. I couldn't, in good conscience, receive communion again until I went, at the very least because I'd skipped Mass the previous Sunday. If I just confessed that I missed Mass, would that cover the entirety of the sin? Then I could avoid going into detail about why I'd missed Mass in the first place. But if someone missed Mass because they had been too busy murdering someone, simply confessing that they had missed Mass would not be sufficient to also receive absolution for the murder. Oh, the joys of being a Catholic who participated in the sacraments. Martin Luther may have had several valid points.

I parked. The next step would be to get out of the car and walk into the church. No big deal.

Get out of the car, Maura. Just don't think about it, I tried to motivate myself.

Really? Not thinking is what got you into this whole mess anyway. You seemed to accomplish NOT thinking pretty successfully last Saturday, my internal lecture continued as I got out and locked my door.

God, what if Ethan was here?

I scanned the parking lot, looking for his car as I made my way into the church. Thankfully, I didn't see it. Although, if he did see me, it would probably help my case for him thinking I wasn't a terrible Catholic. He might even assume I was seeking forgiveness for all the babies I had inadvertently killed by voting for pro-choice candidates and turning a blind eye when Sydney gave girls information about how to get birth control.

Why do I even still care? Wait. Should I confess all that stuff too?

I mulled over all the grey areas that Ethan would probably judge me for. It was easier to examine my conscience regarding that instead of what had happened with Thomas. Sydney's unwelcome analysis on Tuesday had loomed in my head all week. It was easy for her to think that I could simply date Thomas regardless of all his shortcomings when it came to faith and spirituality; people who weren't religious would never understand why that mattered in a relationship.

Then again, I had made it the priority with every guy I had dated for the past ten years and it didn't seem to be yielding very positive results. Had the past ten years all been a sign that I was destined for religious life? Oh great, another thought to obsess over while I stood in line.

The wait seemed to take forever even though there were only four people in front of me. I was upset at the people who showed up for confession that day. Honestly, if it was going to take more than five minutes, they really should've scheduled an appointment for a different time. Then again, I might be able to get absolution without having to physically confess anything if time ran out before the Saturday vigil Mass. I had heard of it happening before, of course at more liberal churches, where the priest had deemed the effort to receive the sacrament enough of a confession in the first place.

I probably would not be so lucky with a priest like Father Jack or Father Bernard behind the confessional door.

I took a deep breath when I finally saw the person ahead of me step out and leave the door open. I stepped in. I was not a fan of the anonymity that came with the old school confession style. Yes, I was one of those hippies who liked receiving the sacrament face to face. It seemed more awkward to talk to a wall. But I really couldn't be picky that night. I closed the door and knelt before the screen. Then I heard the last voice on the planet I wanted to hear.

"In the name of the Father, and the Son, and the Holy Spirit," Sean started.

"Are you kidding me?" I said in whispered exclamation.

He paused.

"Seriously?" I lamented. "What are you doing here?" I demanded, still maintaining my hushed tone.

"Father Bernard had to visit his sister in Kansas, so they asked me to fill in," he explained.

I let out a sigh.

"This is wrong on so many levels."

There had to be some policy written somewhere that forbade priests from hearing their ex-girlfriend's confession.

"Well, then stop taking up other people's time," he said matter-of-factly.

I didn't move, but also didn't say anything.

"You know it's the same sacrament no matter who administers it."

A brief silence passed. I tried to determine how badly I wanted absolution that night. "Just start with any of the commandments that have been broken," he coached.

I remained silent.

"Are you really here to waste my time with the venial stuff?" he attempted to joke.

"I didn't go to Mass last Sunday," I finally confessed. That would be sufficient, given the circumstances. God would understand. I should get points just for being here.

"And what kept you from Mass?"

Damn it.

"What does that matter?" I challenged. I never thought I would find myself bickering with a priest during Reconciliation. Yet another sin against me.

"Context is everything. You know that. If you missed Mass because you had to go see someone in the hospital or your car broke down, obviously that's not something that needs to be reconciled," he explained what I already knew.

"I wasn't in a space to go to Mass."

"Because..." he continued to probe.

"Because I slept with Thomas, okay?" I blurted.

He was silent.

"I mean, I didn't sleep with him, as in have sex, but I fell asleep with him...after we..."

"Okay, I get it," he stopped me before I started describing more.

"Clearly you see why this is awkward," I muttered.

"Oh, I highly doubt you'd be more comfortable talking to Father Bernard about this," he argued. I could picture his stupid, know-it-all smirk.

"Fine. I get it; I'm a horrible slut. There's no need to shame me anymore than I've already done."

"Whoa, I did not say that. Nor do I think that in the least," he clarified.

There was a lull.

"What were your intentions?"

"My intentions?" I asked with confusion.

"Yeah, your intentions. Was it purely physical or was it misguided affection?"

"I don't know. It's doesn't matter."

"Well you know that I know that this whole purity thing can be extremely challenging...especially if you care about the other person." He paused. "Do you care about him?"

I sat there in silence, staring at the screen.

"Maura?"

"You know, I don't think how I feel about him has anything to do with it. A sin is a sin is a sin." Defensive righteousness seemed to be my go-to response in relation to Thomas these days.

"Well, that doesn't sound like you at all," he laughed quietly. His lightheartedness annoyed me.

"You know this whole setup is supposed to be anonymous," I deflected. "You're really just supposed to let the confessor state their sins, give the penance and absolution, and be done with it. If I wanted counseling, I would pay for it."

"Fair point." His tone was calm. "Is there anything else you'd like to confess that can't wait until your standard annual trip to the Lenten reconciliation service in the spring?" he said dryly, knowing I didn't regularly receive the sacrament. I pursed my lips.

"No, I'm good, thanks," I responded pointedly.

He waited a moment.

"Do you still know the prayer of Saint Jude?"

"Yes," I answered with annoyance. Was he being smart in asking me? As if I had fallen from grace so much that I wouldn't remember one of my favorite prayers?

"Okay, your penance is the prayer of Saint Jude."

"Excuse me, are you saying I'm a lost cause?" I asked, offended, even though that was pretty much what I'd been thinking about myself ever since Ethan had broken up with me.

Sean sighed. "No, but you're clearly frustrated with yourself and projecting it onto me, which gives me the sense that Saint Jude's intercession could be of some use to you. Are you ready for your act of contrition?"

I stated the Act of Contrition from memory, thankful that the interaction with Sean was almost over, but feeling a pang of guilt over how short I had been with him. When I was done, he proclaimed that Jesus had absolved me of my sins and closed with the sign of the cross.

"Maura?" He stopped me as I stood up to leave. "God doesn't expect you to be perfect, especially when it comes to love...try to offer the same grace to yourself...and maybe also to certain individuals who are fairly new to the concept." He seemed to be alluding to Thomas, but how could he know, since I hadn't told him anything about what Thomas had said to me that morning in my apartment. I left without responding, unsure of what to make of Sean's last-ditch effort to give me advice.

Knowing I should complete my penance before leaving the church, I walked over and knelt before the shrine of Saint Jude. I stared at the statue. Whether I liked it or not, it would forever be connected to Thomas because of the painting he had given me. I started mumbling the prayer quietly to myself.

"O most holy apostle, Saint Jude, faithful servant and friend of Jesus, the Church honors and invokes thee universally, as the patron of hopeless cases, and of things almost despaired of. Pray for me, who am so miserable. Make use, I implore thee, of that particular privilege accorded to thee, to bring visible and speedy help where help was almost despaired of. Come to mine assistance in this great need, that I may receive the consolation and succor of Heaven in all my necessities, tribulations, and sufferings, particularly..."

I paused. I did not know how to verbalize what exactly I was praying for. My mind flooded with all the memories of the past five years. I felt lonely...unlovable...and overwhelmingly flawed. Before I knew it, tears were falling down my cheeks. I didn't try to define it with words, but just sat there, finally acknowledging how much I had been hurting ever since things had fallen apart with Sean.

Ever since he'd left me, I hadn't really trusted in the possibility that any man could ever truly love me. Silently, I pleaded not to feel the emptiness and doubt in my heart anymore as the tears continued to flow. Once I gathered a little bit more composure I continued, "...and that I may praise God with thee and all the elect throughout eternity. I promise thee, O blessed Jude, to be ever mindful of this great favor, to always honor thee as my special and powerful patron, and to gratefully encourage devotion to thee. Amen."

I wiped the tears off my cheeks and casually looked around to ensure there was no one I knew in the chapel before getting up. The last thing I wanted was to have to explain to someone why I'd been crying. Thankfully, I didn't see anyone I knew, so I didn't have to think of a lie in case I was asked.

Great, Maura, you just went to confession, and your first instinct is to lie if someone asks you why you're crying, I reprimanded myself. *Should I stay for Mass? No, I just want to go home and not think about all of this.*

As I walked through the parking lot, a familiar truck caught the corner of my eye. It was an old, white, Chevy truck. It had to be

Thomas', but it didn't make sense that Thomas would be here. He was the last person on Earth who would go to confession.

I tried to recall all the people I'd seen inside the chapel, struggling to remember if any of them looked like Thomas from behind or from a distance. The thought of running into him after refusing to answer any of his calls or texts was enough to get me into my car and out of the parking lot at top speed.

Could I really have feelings for Thomas O'Hollaren? Actual feelings that went beyond physical attraction? Was that even possible? If I did, it absolutely terrified me because I knew it would only lead to getting hurt...again. I mean, if I couldn't make it work with guys who had the same faith as me, then it definitely wouldn't work with someone who had absolutely no faith in anything.

Once I made it home, I sought my usual strategy for avoidance and denial; reality TV. But unfortunately, I didn't have a DVR, which meant I had to sit through all the commercials, including the one for Saint Jude's Children's hospital that played six times within a thirty-minute time frame, even though I changed the channel three times. I tried to avoid it, to ignore the association, but there it was on every channel. It was like I couldn't get away from it.

Maura, you've seen this commercial plenty of times before. You're just sensitive to it now because stupid Sean had you say the prayer of Saint Jude. There is no supernatural, spiritual intervention occurring. God is way too busy with real problems to have time for your petty shit.

However, after it played for the tenth time, I decided it was weird and switched to Netflix.

I successfully distracted myself with a long awaited *Breaking Bad* binge, then called it a night and went to bed. Even though it was late, I still found myself tossing and turning. When I was little, my mom taught me a trick to help me when I couldn't fall asleep: pray the rosary. The alternative was lying there and thinking about Thomas, which would ultimately lead to thinking about making out with him, which would lead to texting him, and that was not in my best interest. I pulled out my rosary from my night stand.

As I said the prayers silently in my head, my mind began to drift back to the prayer of Saint Jude. Halfway through, I stopped saying the prayers that made up the rosary, which I'm sure is something a good Catholic is not supposed to do, and started praying the prayer of Saint Jude instead. I had never in my life felt compelled to recite any specific prayer over another, but in that moment that was the only way I could describe it. After I finished it, I soon drifted peacefully off to sleep.

That was the way it went every night that week. I would begin each night feeling restless lying in bed, trying to fall asleep, and then I would say the Prayer of Saint Jude and suddenly feel relaxed enough to drift off. It wasn't until Wednesday that I realized I had started a novena to Saint Jude. I hadn't prayed a novena since undergrad, so I was curious to see if anything would come from it. The ability to fall asleep soundly was more than enough of a benefit for me at that point.

Maybe it was all psychosomatic, but in addition to being able to sleep better, I started to feel more at peace when it came to being myself, and feel more open to my future. I didn't need to be with Ethan to be a good Catholic, and just because we saw the world differently, it didn't make me a bad Catholic or unlovable. I deserved to be with someone who didn't leave me second-guessing everything about myself. Also helping with my newfound inner peace was that Thomas had stopped calling me and Sydney had left for vacation so she wasn't around to offer her two cents. It was a relief that I didn't have to try and figure out what the whole thing with Thomas meant – if it meant anything at all.

In fact, I felt so grounded and peaceful that I agreed to go to nine o'clock Sunday Mass with my parents that weekend. It had crossed my mind that Thomas would potentially be there, but I figured since I had turned him down, he would have stopped attending church all together. Yeah, that was kind of egotistical... and wrong.

All that tranquility I had built up over the week escaped me when I saw Thomas walk in with his family. My heart raced and my palms started to sweat. Almost compulsively, I found myself reciting the Prayer of Saint Jude in my head, hoping it would offer the same results as before.

Why the hell am I so flustered? He hasn't even looked at me, I mused to myself.

Because you love him.

No, I don't, I argued. *That doesn't make sense. I need to find a nice boy who goes to church.*

He's at church right now, isn't he?

Ugh. Shut up, brain.

It made absolutely no sense why I would still allow myself to be attracted to Thomas. Having any sort of romantic relationship with him that ended happily seemed near impossible...so why even go down that road?

THOMAS

Maura was sitting next to her parents when I walked into the church. It had been two weeks since I last saw her and fucked everything up. Michael had advised me to give her some space until I knew exactly what I wanted to say. Of course, a week had passed and I still had no clue what I would say to her if I had the opportunity. Father Sean and Michael expected that I would somehow become brave enough to tell her that I loved her, but I had my doubts. All I wanted was to go back to a time when I could make her laugh.

Before mass started, I tried several times to make eye contact with her, which was difficult to do, at least nonchalantly, given that I was sitting up at the front with my family. She didn't do me any favors by looking everywhere but in my direction. I spent the entirety of the readings and the homily trying to figure out exactly what I was going to say to Maura at the end of mass. Everything I came up with was either insufficiently superficial or terrifyingly honest.

Mass seemed to take forever. Maura didn't go up for communion. Was that to avoid being near me? When the service finally concluded, she was already halfway to the back exit by the time I turned around. Her walk was quicker than any other time I had seen her rush out of church before. It wasn't like I had figured out what I was going to say to her anyway.

My family lingered on the front lawn after the service. Chris and Michael were discussing something to do with Chris' firm. Margaret was making plans with another family. I stared off into space.

Should I have chased after her? Seriously pursuing a woman was so unfamiliar to me. How much effort was I supposed to put in before taking a hint and moving on?

The parking lot gradually emptied as cars exited. Just as a black sedan cleared away, I saw her standing by her car.

"Looks like she's got a flat," Michael observed, calling me out of my head. "If that's not an opportunity to start to redeem yourself, I don't know what is."

I didn't argue, but he sensed my hesitation.

"Go."

I knew from his tone that my fear of rejection would be an insufficient excuse.

She had already gotten her spare tire and car jack out. She was wearing a skirt, which I assumed had led her to delay the process, not wanting to bend over too far or kneel on the ground in a crowded parking lot.

"Need some help?" I called.

She looked up.

"I know how to change a tire," she answered abruptly.

"I know. I taught you."

She ignored me and tried to position herself while maintaining modesty. I walked over and held my hand out for the wrench.

"No need to get your skirt dirty...or you know, flash all the God-fearing folk."

Maura didn't smile like I hoped she would. Instead, she handed off the wrench, not bothering to look at me.

"I'm surprised your parents left you here stranded. It's so unlike Laura and James to abandon their only child," I said dryly, flipping my tie over my shoulder while I bent down to remove the lug nuts.

"I didn't walk out with them," she explained. "I was trying to get out of here before–"

"You had to talk to me," I filled in.

"I have a lot of things to do today." She brushed off my attempt to hook her. I placed the jack under the car and started to lift it.

"Well hello, Maura," my mom approached us. "I see you've had a bit of bad luck this morning. I'm glad Tommy is able to help you out."

Maura smiled politely. It wasn't her real smile.

"You can go ahead without me. Maura can give me a ride home after I fix this at the shop," I informed without asking Maura her thoughts on the matter.

"All right. Maura, you should join us for dinner tonight if you don't have any plans." Maura opened her mouth, getting ready to decline the offer.

"She says she has a lot to do today."

"Oh, that's too bad. But it's no problem if you change your mind; just let Tommy know," my mom said hopefully before walking to her car.

"Thank you," Maura said. She waited until my mom was out of earshot. "I really don't need you to fix it today. It can sit in my garage the rest of the day."

"Thought you had a lot of things to do today?" I challenged.

She clenched her jaw. "At home. I have a lot of things to do at home. I can take the car in tomorrow morning."

"Oh, you mean, first thing, when I won't be there?" I attempted to tease, but it sounded more combative than I wanted it to. "We have a pretty packed schedule tomorrow at the shop. I'd rather just get it done now."

"You're assuming I'm taking it to you?"

"Well, what other shop bills your dad for all the work on your car?"

She was visibly annoyed that I knew this about her. Again, my teasing came across more like being an asshole. Fuck. I lowered the car and placed the flat and the jack in her trunk. I held out my hands for her keys. The last time I did this, she'd been a lot happier to be around me.

"I am perfectly capable of driving," she declared, moving to the driver's door.

"Okay, then," I said, calmly moving to the passenger's seat.

We drove in silence. She didn't even have the radio on as a buffer. After fifteen minutes, I couldn't take it anymore.

"So, what's new? How have you been?" I asked cheerfully. Maybe if I acted like nothing was wrong, things could just go back to normal. I mean, we didn't have to talk about what happened, right? Or the fact that for the past fourteen days, all I had been able to think about was what her hair smelled like and that I missed her smile. What the hell was happening to me?

"I'm fine." She offered nothing more. We relapsed into silent tension. I had never been more relieved to pull up to the shop.

"Be right back." I opened the garage and waved her over to the lift. She got out of the car and started walking away without saying anything.

"Where are you going?"

She stopped and turned around. "The waiting room. Isn't that where I'm supposed to go?"

"Only during business hours. I mean, unless you really don't want to stay here and keep me company...while I work on your car...on my day off."

She crossed her arms. "You're the one who insisted we come here now."

"Well, how else am I supposed to spend time with you if you won't return my calls?" I tried to sound like I was joking, but we both knew I was being honest. She looked down at her feet. Okay, so maybe I couldn't act like nothing happened. I loosened my tie and removed it.

"I didn't think it was a good idea for us to hang out after–"

"You rejected me," I filled in, now unbuttoning my shirt.

"I did not reject you," she quickly countered, looking back up at me.

"Hmm..." I pretended to think. "I said I was interested in you and you told me that you don't date guys like me. Sounds like rejection to me." I pulled my shirt off, still wearing an undershirt.

She looked away again.

"Don't worry, that's all the clothing I plan on removing." I draped my shirt and tie on a nearby counter.

She let out a frustrated sigh, obviously not enjoying our exchange. I wasn't either. How could someone go from being the friendliest person I'd ever met to the absolute coldest? It was bizarre; normally, if someone infuriated me this much, I would happily avoid them. But there she was, pissing me off, and all I wanted to do was kiss her and let her know how much I wanted her – to convince her how good I could be for her if she just let me.

Her cheeks were flushed from the humidity, triggering the memory of what she'd looked like when we spent the night together,

"The AC's off since we're usually not here at this time," I explained awkwardly, trying not to stare at her. "The office actually stays pretty cool if you want to wait in there," I offered, thinking of a way to avoid ogling her. "This shouldn't take too long."

She nodded and walked toward the office without a word. I shifted my focus to something I could control: fixing the damn tire. She had driven over a nail and the tear was too deep to repair. Over the course of putting on the new tire, I concluded that even if I wasn't sorry about what had happened, I would need to apologize to her and accept that she would never feel the same about me. Maybe someday I could work my way back to being her friend. I'd rather have that than not have her in my life at all.

MAURA

I sighed once inside Thomas' office. I had no idea how to act around him anymore and desperately wanted things to go back to how they were before. My icy demeanor wasn't helping matters any. At least the office was a few degrees cooler, like he had said. Maybe physically cooling down would help me be less agitated.

To distract myself, I looked over some photos pinned on the wall behind one of the desks. They were of Michael's sons. I walked over to the other desk, presumably Thomas'. The ridiculous unicorn picture I had given him was propped up in the corner. There was a framed picture of the voc-ed group next to it. Sydney and I had given him the picture as a thank you, but I hadn't given much thought as to whether he would display it, much like when I'd given him that silly paint-by-number picture. But there they both were.

He had two other pictures up on the wall. I recognized that they were taken on Easter. In one, he was standing with his mother, and in the other he was helping his nieces look for Easter eggs. Who would've guessed he'd be so sentimental?

The desk was extremely well organized, another unexpected discovery. There was a piece of paper with a handwritten list in the corner near the tacky unicorn picture. I started reading the items listed, quickly realizing that it had nothing to do with his work at the shop.

The Sound on a sunny day

The ocean

The rain

When it snows

Hitting a home run

Baseball

Hunter, Andrew, Gabriel, James, Sophie, Grace

My mother

My mother's cooking

Wine

Beer

Sleeping

Painting

About halfway down the page, I saw my name. Even though I knew I had no right to be snooping through his things, I picked up the paper to see what else he had written, mostly interested in finding out if there was anything else about me.

Maura

Her smile

Her laugh

Caring

Innocence

Passionate

Her horrible jokes

Ridiculous taste in music

Kind

Intelligent

Talented

Faithful

Beautiful

Determined

"So, I'm finished with the tire."

I froze. Thomas was standing in the doorway of the office.

"But it looks like your alignment is off again. Are you really in that big of a hurry to get back home, or do you mind if I just fix that now? Normally I would've just done that first but I didn't know how long you were willing to wait."

I stood there, too stunned to fully process his question.

I turned around, still holding the list, accepting that I had been caught. He looked at me with confusion. Then he looked down to see what I was holding.

"Oh," he started and then stopped. We both stood there silently. He rubbed the back of his neck; he did that whenever he was nervous.

"So," he sighed. "I, uh...went to confession last Saturday...and my penance was to make a list of everything I was thankful for..." he explained.

"You went to confession?" I knew I had seen his truck on Saturday but was still shocked to hear him say he'd actually received the sacrament.

"Yep," he said. "Broke my eighteen-year streak."

"Why?"

"Uh, well," he paused. "Father Sean suggested it might help my chances with you," he admitted.

I looked back down at the paper, letting his words sink in.

"Which," he sighed, "now sounds really manipulative."

"Do you believe in God?" I blurted. I had always assumed he didn't believe in anything.

"Yes...I mean, I think I do..."

I stared at him, searching.

"Look, Maura, I don't want to stand here and pretend like the whole faith thing comes as easily for me as it does for you. I've always been a skeptic with just about everything. And that's probably a big reason why you're not interested in me," he reasoned. Then he looked me in the eye. "But what I can honestly tell you is that knowing you and what your faith means to you makes me believe in God more than I ever did before. Who knows? Maybe that was Father Sean's whole point in having me make the list in the first place: to recognize that all of the great things in my life have to come from somewhere."

"I'm one of the great things in your life?" I clarified.

Thomas laughed.

"Did you not notice that the list just turns into a list of reasons why I love you?"

Once the words came out, I could tell by his expression that he hadn't meant to tell me that.

"You love me?"

Thomas took a deep breath.

"I...I know things went too far for you the other night...and I'm sorry that ended up being so upsetting for you...but I'm not sorry it happened," he said. "You have to believe me when I tell you that I've never done anything like that before and had it mean as much to me as it did with you. I've never been in love before...it always seemed like too much work...but..." he paused and rubbed the back of his neck again, "Maura, being around you has never felt like work...yet I've never worked harder in my life to make myself a better person...and I don't not want to be around you...shit," he sighed and shook his head. "This isn't coming out right at all," he fumbled. "What I mean is—"

Before he could finish, I walked over and kissed him. It was the first time I'd ever initiated a kiss, at least a kiss that really meant something. Everything I had felt the first time I kissed him was still there, possibly more so now that I knew how much he cared about me. He kissed me back, relieved that he didn't have to keep trying to explain himself. After a few moments, I broke away.

"I'm sorry," I finally apologized.

"Wait, are you rejecting me again? After kissing me like that?" he said with disbelief.

"No, no," I quickly corrected. "I'm sorry for the other night. I took advantage of you and–"

Thomas started laughing.

"What?"

He shook his head. "Nothing. I'm just glad you're finally accepting responsibility for taking advantage of this poor unsuspecting Catholic boy."

"Unsuspecting? Let's not push it," I warned. "You kissed me first."

"After you lured me back to your apartment and put on booty shorts," he argued.

"I did not–"

He stopped me, pulling me in closer to kiss me again.

"You realize your penance was pretty much to play The Glad Game, don't you?" I pointed out, happy to finally smile with him again.

"Well, I guess Pollyanna wasn't as irrelevant as I had judged her to be."

"So," I took a step back, holding up the paper and pretending to examine it. "I'm just curious to see if 'Maura not putting out' made it on the list?" I wanted to make sure he knew my position on the matter hadn't changed, regardless of how much I liked kissing him.

"This is a living document," he responded coolly, taking the paper from me. "I feel like I'd have to be your boyfriend to fully appreciate just how much you don't put out."

"Are you saying you want to be my boyfriend?"

"Well, I am in love you," he said matter-of-factly.

"You're sure? Even with no sex?" I reiterated. "Not even the stuff we did the other night; that's included. I mean, I don't want you thinking that's par for the course, even though I let it happen the one time," I started to ramble. He reached out and grabbed my hand, again pulling me closer to him, looking me in the eye.

"Even with no sex," he confirmed. "Just lots of kissing and hand holding." He wrapped his arms around me. "And the occasional ass-grab and boob play. You know, just to keep it romantic," he added with a grin.

I rolled my eyes and kissed him again. He was the last thing I had expected and it still terrified me. There were still a lot of unknowns and challenges that would come with dating him. But as I stood there being held by him, it was the first time I felt like someone loved me entirely for who I was and not for what he wanted me to be. Of all people, he gave me hope that loving me wasn't such a lost cause after all. I would do the same for him.